Mary Margaret

Meets Her Match

Also by
CHRISTINE KOLE MACLEAN

Mary Margaret and the Perfect Pet Plan

Mary Margaret, Center Stage

Mary Margaret

Meets Her Match

by Christine Kole MacLean

Dutton
Children's
Books

DUTTON CHILDREN'S BOOKS
A division of Penguin Young Readers Group
Published by the Penguin Group • Penguin Group (USA) Inc., 375 Hudson
Street, New York, New York 10014, U.S.A. • Penguin Group (Canada),
90 Eglinton Avenue East, Suite 700, Toronto, Ontario, Canada M4P 2Y3
(a division of Pearson Penguin Canada Inc.) • Penguin Books Ltd,
80 Strand, London WC2R 0RL, England • Penguin Ireland,
25 St Stephen's Green, Dublin 2, Ireland (a division of Penguin Books Ltd) •
Penguin Group (Australia), 250 Camberwell Road, Camberwell, Victoria
3124, Australia (a division of Pearson Australia Group Pty Ltd) • Penguin
Books India Pvt Ltd, 11 Community Centre, Panchsheel Park, New Delhi -
110 017, India • Penguin Group (NZ), Cnr Airborne and Rosedale Roads,
Albany, Auckland 1310, New Zealand (a division of Pearson New Zealand
Ltd) • Penguin Books (South Africa) (Pty) Ltd, 24 Sturdee Avenue,
Rosebank, Johannesburg 2196, South Africa • Penguin Books Ltd,
Registered Offices: 80 Strand, London WC2R 0RL, England

The publisher does not have any control over and does not assume any
responsibility for author or third-party websites or their content.

CIP Data is available.

Published in the United States by Dutton Children's Books,
a division of Penguin Young Readers Group,
345 Hudson Street, New York, New York 10014
www.penguin.com/youngreaders

Designed by IRENE VANDERVOORT

Printed in USA   First Edition

10 9 8 7 6 5 4 3 2 1   ISBN 978-0-525-47775-4

For Wendy, who will always be Wendie to me

Acknowledgments

Thank you, Chris Hart and Mary Kit Rice at the Double JJ
Ranch, Angie Barnes (and B.) at Top Crest Stable, and
everyone at Juniper Hill Farm for letting me hang around. Any
horse-related mistakes I may have made are my fault, not theirs.
Stacy Morgan, thanks for the worries.
Stephanie Owens Lurie, you are still helping me find my seat
as a writer, and I'm so grateful for your patience.
Thank you, Ramon F. Adams, author of *Cowboy Lingo*,
where I found many of the cowboy expressions used herein.
Madeline and Clark, thanks for the most thrilling ride of all!

Contents

1. Dream On   3

2. Terco Time   18

3. Giddyup!   30

4. Kan't-sas   42

5. Baby, I'm Blue   59

6. Goose, Goose . . . Duck!   67

7. Unfamiliar Territory   75

8. Poop-Out at the Old Corral   84

9. I Make My Own Party   98

10. Breaking Away   112

11. I Am in So Much Trouble   128

12. Rider No-Show-Off   135

13. What I Got Out of It   146

Mary Margaret

Meets Her Match

I haven't beat the waffles yet, but this morning, things are going to be different. This morning, I'm going to show them that I am the queen of them.

It's our new toaster's fault the waffles don't already know I'm the queen. My dad says the toaster has a bad attitude. Instead of popping the frozen waffles up when they are done, it flings the waffles up, which always scares my baby sister, Liza, and makes her cry. I think the flinging and soaring makes the waffles think they can be free. If the waffles were animals, I'd help them. But they are just waffles.

My dad thinks it's funny. He stops the waffles by putting his hand above the toaster just before they are done, so they rebound off his hand and land right back in the toaster. "Back where you belong!" he says.

My mom thinks it's annoying. She just lets them land wherever and then says, "They can make cell phones that take pictures but they can't make a toaster that works right."

For me it's a game—me against the waffles—and I try to catch them on my plate. I've almost done it a few times, but the waffles always *bump bibble bobble* off the plate. I'm not sure, but I think they might be laughing at me, and I hate being laughed at.

So breakfast time is crazy at my house, with Liza busting out crying every time the toaster hurls waffles, and the waffles trying to escape so they don't get eaten, and all of us grabbing at them. All of us except my older brother, JT, who doesn't even like waffles.

JT is thirteen and most of the time acts like he's too cool to care. But sometimes he can still be really fun. Like yesterday, when he pretended he was a sportscaster talking about a game, which is pretty funny because he doesn't even like sports much. He even made up a name for the person trying to catch the waffles—plate-ster. "And the waffles are in the air, folks!" he said, using his spoon as a pretend microphone. "The plate-ster goes right . . . but the waffle fakes left and the plate-ster misses completely. She dives for the other waffle and slams into the counter! Oooo! Uhhh! That's gotta hurt!"

"JT!" I said. "You bent my concentration." Actually, I like it when JT does stuff like that, but I wouldn't ever tell him.

This morning, though, JT isn't even watching. He's just staring into his bowl of Cheerios acting like he's mad about something. I check in with my memory to see if there's anything I did to make him mad. My memory says just one thing, and it's not something JT could know about because I got away with it. A few days ago I went into his room when he wasn't there and hid under his bed. I knew I shouldn't, but I just wanted to know what he does in there with the door closed. The answer to that is, nothing very interesting. Or maybe he did do interesting stuff and I just couldn't tell because all I could see were his feet.

Anyway, after a while I started to get the giggles because those feet looked like they weren't attached to legs and I started thinking of them as the Feetie family and making up stories about all the adventures they were having now that they didn't have to listen to the legs. I closed my eyes to take my mind off the Feetie family, and then it was so boring that I almost fell asleep.

I'm pretty sure JT doesn't know about any of that because I was very quiet and didn't crawl out from under the bed until he went downstairs. So JT must be mad at somebody else, which is good news for me.

I put the waffles into the toaster, pick up my plate, and stare at the slots. I concentrate so hard, I don't even blink. I hardly even breathe. I'm ready. Today is going to be the day that I finally do it. The toaster makes a ticking sound as it heats the waffles up. Almost done . . . any minute . . . any second. My muscles are on alert, ready for anything . . . ready . . . readier . . .

POP!

The waffles whoosh by me. My body doesn't wait for my brain to tell it what to do. My arm shoots to the right.

I catch one waffle as it starts to come back down. It lands on the center of the plate. For once it stays there. I flick the plate to the left—too fast! The waffle bounces off the rim, but—lucky me!—it gives a little hop up. I have another chance to get under it. I drop to my knees (ouch!). I shove the plate under the falling waffle—just in time.

"I did it!" I shout. "Look! Look! I did it! Now I can add this to my list of things I admire about myself."

My mom claps and says, "That list must be getting pretty long."

"It is!" I say. "I have them all memorized. There's my fashion style, my recipes for interesting lunches, my poems, my understanding of animals, my cartwheels, my—"

"Humility," interrupts JT.

"I don't get embarrassed," I say.

"Humility, not humiliated," my mom says. "Humility is the opposite of being proud. JT's being sarcastic, but never mind him. I think it's good to have things you admire about yourself."

I give JT a dirty look and start to say more things that are on my list, but right then the second miracle of the day happens. Liza—the crybaby in our family—actually smiles. "Look! She's smiling!"

JT puts his bowl in the dishwasher. "It's just gas," he says.

He wants to spoil my good feeling, but I want to hang on to it. "Even if it is, I still caught the waffles, and that was pretty great."

"Way to go," he says in his most bored voice. "You're a regular *waffle wrangler*." Then he looks at my mom like there's a whole bunch more he wants to say to her.

"JT," she says, and she looks at him like there's more she wants to say to him. This time, I know what it is. It's "change your attitude."

At least now I know who JT is mad at, and it's not me. Since it's not me, I ask, "What's wrong?"

"There's a snake in my boot," says JT.

My mom holds him by the shoulders and steers him out of the kitchen. "You'll be late for school if you don't get moving." JT goes without even saying good-bye.

Later, when I leave for the bus stop, I feel happy about the waffles but a little sad, too. I think about that for a minute—what's there to feel sad about? Then I figure out it's because the rest of my day will be boring compared to the *glory* of catching those waffles. *Glory* is one of our vocabulary words. It means "shining achievement." I like that word—*glory*. I also like the word *glorious*, which means "magnificent" and "wonderful."

"Mary Margaret!" my mom calls out our front door.

I turn around.

"I forgot to tell you that I'll pick you up from school today. We have some shopping to do."

I groan. I am not a champion at shopping. Pet shopping is the best, but we've only done that once, when we picked out Hershey, my pet rabbit. Grocery shopping is all right because it's pretty fast and I like to watch the lobsters in their tank.

Maybe it's shopping for new furniture. At least when we do that kind of shopping I get to flop down on all the beds and crank the footstools on the recliner chairs—all of them. My mom said that to me once. "Do you have to try every single one?" And I told her yes. Otherwise how would I know which one is best? And she said that we weren't even shopping for recliners. And then I said that I was just working ahead of the family, just like sometimes I work ahead of the class at school, and that when we did want to buy a recliner, I would know exactly which one to buy. And after that, she didn't say anything.

"What kind of shopping?" I yell.

"Clothes shopping," she says.

I hang my head and start walking again toward the bus stop. Clothes shopping is the worst kind of shopping of all! I hate clothes shopping because all my mom and me do is fight, fight, fight.

"It'll be fun!" she yells.

"About as fun as getting a shot on a sunburned arm," I say to the sidewalk. I know she can't hear me, but she must be squinting hard enough to read my mind, even though I'm a block away from her.

"Hippopotamus!" she shouts.

I spin around, zippety fast. "We're going shopping for a *hippopotamus*?"

"No! I said, 'I PROMISE!'"

I slump away. I've never shopped for a hippopotamus before. For a second, I had thought that shopping really would be fun.

Once I get on the bus, things get better for me again. I tell my best friend Andy all about how I caught the waffles. And once I'm at school, I tell my friend Ellie about it, too, only this time I act it out. Ellie and I were in a play together once, so I have a lot of practice at acting. I do such a good job of acting it out that pretty soon everybody is watching me and laughing.

Then my teacher, Mr. Mooney, comes into the class-room and I think he's going to be mad at me because I have this teeny problem about not being able to stay in my seat. And we have had a few little chats about that. Instead, he asks me to do it again so he can see. Everyone applauds and then Mr. Mooney says, "Okay, class, now it really is time to get to work," and so we all do. But still, starting the day like that was a happiness, and I forget all about the shopping trip.

The first thing we do is take our math test. It's the kind of test where you have to see how many problems you can get done in four minutes. We do these every Friday, which today is. The very first time I took the test, I got all one hundred problems done, so I thought I'd passed the test. I even thought I might be a math whiz! But then Mr. Mooney said the answers all have to be *right*, which I didn't think was fair because it's like taking two tests at once—one for how fast you are and one for how good you are.

Mr. Mooney says to practice every day after school. I would rather help my rabbit Hershey practice tricks. She already comes when I call her and now I'm trying to teach her to play ball. What I'd really like is a dog, but my dad is allergic to animal fur so instead we got a rabbit and she stays outside in a hutch. I don't tell Hershey that I wish she was a dog. Hershey loves me and would do anything for me, but no matter how much she wants to, she can't change into a dog.

"Ready?" Mr. Mooney asks. I grip my pencil and nod, thinking that I might as well just get it over with. "Then you may begin."

Even numbers are my favorite, so I do them first. I make up a little poem about them.

> *Two, four,*
> *Six, eight, ten,*
> *No other numbers*
> *Make better friends!*

By the time I'm done with the even numbers, I notice the odd numbers are scowling at me. Maybe they just feel left out. So I make up a poem about them and whisper it.

> *One, three,*
> *Five, seven, nine,*
> *They look sharp and mean*
> *But I heard that they are kind!*

I start liking the odd numbers a little better and maybe they like me a little better, too, because suddenly they are adding and subtracting themselves in my brain just like the even numbers do.

After the time is up, we correct our tests and . . . I pass! I jump up and do a happy wriggle dance next to my desk. It goes like this: "I passed!"—wriggle my botto, wriggle my botto—"I passed!"—poke my finger up high, poke my finger down low. "Oh, yeah, I passed!"—last botto wriggle and two big hops.

I know that Mr. Mooney is going to tell me, "Please, Mary Margaret, sit down, didn't we just talk about this and you must learn to stay in your seat!" I am so happy the odd numbers and I are friends that I don't care. Mr. Mooney doesn't say any of those things, though. He just smiles, shakes his head, and says, "Today must be your day, Mary Margaret."

He's right. Today *is* my day. Because at lunch, after I eat my lasagna sandwich, Granny Smith apple, key-lime yogurt, and carrot-cake cupcake, I notice there is still something. It's way down deep in the bottom of my bag, under my napkin (which I never take out because I am a very neat eater, usually). I reach in and pull it out. It's a package of Twinkies. Taped to it is a note from my dad. *Happy Double Dessert Day, Mary Margaret!* it says.

Ellie leans over and reads the note. "What's Double Dessert Day?"

"Something my dad does sometimes," I say, pulling open the wrapper. I give her one of the Twinkies.

"Thanks," she says, all happy. She eats it in tiny bites. She carefully wipes her fingers and mouth with the damp towel-thingy that her mother always puts in her lunch. Ellie is a neater eater than I am, but you can't ever be too neat or clean for Ellie's mom. "How does he decide which days are Double Dessert Days?"

I shrug. "He's only done it once before, and that was when . . ." Suddenly I feel a little sick to my stomach.

"When what?"

"Ooh," I groan. "Oh no, no, no. They promised. They promised Liza was *it*!"

"What are you talking about?"

"The only other time Dad packed double dessert was on the day my mom and dad told me they were having another baby."

"So you think this means . . . ?"

"Maybe—but they promised!" I hug my stomach and bend over a little. "Ooooo, I don't feel so well."

McKenzie, this other girl in my class, leans across the table and holds out her hand. "Then can I have that other Twinkie?"

"No," I say, sitting up quickly and stuffing the soft, sweet cake into my mouth. I'm not feeling *that* sick.

When my mom drives up in our minivan, I slide open the door. As usual, Baby Liza is in her car seat, which I'm going to have to climb over like I always do. She frowns her baby frown at me and gives her pacifier a slurpy suck. I just stand there. "Well?" I say.

My mom twists around and looks at me over the top of her sunglasses. "Are you going to get in?" she asks. She has a funny look on her face, like she's excited about something and trying not to smile. How can she be excited about having another baby when the one we've got gets in the way all the time?

I put my hand on my hip and say, "When's the due date?" The due date is the day that the baby is supposed to be born, only babies don't always cooperate. I learned that the last time my mom had a baby.

"Due date?" She looks confused. I guess she didn't think I was smart enough to figure out the clues. Her funny smile. Double Dessert Day. Clothes shopping—for her, of course. For those ugly pregnant-lady clothes.

I close my eyes and sigh. "It's easier on me if you just give it to me straight." That's something I heard in a movie once.

"There is no due date that I'm aware of," she says.

I squint at her, trying to decide if she's telling the one hundred percent truth. "We're not going shopping for pregnant clothes?"

"No. What gave you that idea?"

So I explain exactly what gave me that idea.

And then my mother bonks her head onto the steering wheel and laughs. She laughs so hard that a tear slides out from under her sunglasses and her nose starts to run. She laughs so hard that it's making me mad.

I stamp my foot, which is my way of saying I don't get what's so funny. "Then what are we going shopping for and why did Dad decide to do Double Dessert Day?"

She wipes her eyes. "I don't know why your father packed an extra dessert. He's just being thoughtful, probably. And about the shopping trip, I wanted to surprise you, but it looks like·I'm going to have to tell you now." I can tell she's trying to serious herself up. "Cowboy boots," she says. "That's what we're going shopping for."

"Cowboy boots? For me?"

"Yes," she says. "Cowboy boots for you."

My mouth drops open because this is a big surprise. I've been saving for cowboy boots for a while, but it is taking too long. Partly because I keep buying other stuff with my money. Lately I've been begging for them. Begging never works at my house, but when it comes to cowboy boots, I can't control myself. My mom would say I'm obsessed, which means I want them so much that I can't think of anything else, only those boots. *Obsessed* is her new favorite word. *Exhausted* is her old favorite word.

"Red ones? With pink tassels?"

"Whatever color you think the horses would like," she says. She's smiling. So are her eyes. I wonder how she gets her eyes to do that.

This little chat is not going exactly the way I thought it

would. In fact, this little chat is getting weird. When I first opened the van door, I was ready to be all-out mad about her having another baby and about going clothes shopping. Now I don't know how to be. I don't even know what she's talking about.

"What horses?"

"The ones at the Lazy K dude ranch where we're all going. One of my clients wants to throw a party at the dude ranch, so we're going to take a working vacation. That means I work and everyone else in the family gets to be on vacation."

Pppppt. Liza spits her pacifier out and it falls onto the carpeting. There's an indent around her mouth from sucking on that thing so hard. I pick it up and pop it back into her mouth before she can start crying. "When?"

"Tomorrow. So get in already and let's go buy those boots!"

"Tomorrow! But why didn't you tell me?"

"I thought it would be a fun surprise—at least for you. I told JT ahead of time because I suspected he might not be thrilled. He's not."

"So that's what he's mad about?" I crawl over Liza and put on my seat belt while Mom tells me everything. And then I tell her all about my day—reminding her about how I caught the waffles and telling her how I passed the timed math test and did a happy dance and Mr. Mooney didn't yell at me once all day, even though I was up out of my seat one or two or maybe even five times when I shouldn't have been and double dessert and now even the shopping trip is turning out to be a good thing.

"And tomorrow we're going to the dude ranch," I say. "That's about six good things—no, wait. The dude ranch should count double, so that's eight good things in one day!

"Hey, wait a minute," I say.

"What?"

"Shhh," I say, because I am thinking something hard and I can't do that and talk at the same time. What I am thinking is that this day is too good to be true. If my day were a math problem, it would look like this: catching waffles + passing math test + not getting yelled at by Mr. Mooney + double dessert + getting cowboy boots + getting to go to dude ranch where there are real live horses that I will get to ride = a perfect day for me. Which means that none of this is really happening at all. I must be having a terrific dream. Good dreams are fun until I wake up, and then they are just a big letdown. But if I was dreaming, then I'd be getting a horse of my own instead of just going to a dude ranch, so something is rotten here.

Then I know what to do to find out if I'm dreaming. "Mom," I say, "can I have a dog?"

"No," she says.

That's what she always says. And this time her saying no makes me really happy. Because it means I'm not dreaming and everything else that happened today is real and true. It is a glorious day and nothing is rotten.

I lean forward so I can shout out my mom's open window. "HEY! I'm going to a dude ranch in my new RED cowboy boots!"

My mom claps one hand over her ear. "Giddyup," she says. But she sounds a little less excited than me. Maybe she needs a pair of red cowboy boots, too.

2. Jerco Time

My mom says that we'll be hitting the dusty trail at the crack of dawn on Saturday, so I decide to sleep in my jeans and T-shirt. That way I won't have to waste time in the morning getting dressed. I don't want my mom to find out, so I pull the covers way up under my chin. "Brrrr!" I say, when she comes in to say good night. I shiver my shoulders. "It sure is chilly tonight!"

"You're not getting sick, are you?" she says, putting her hand on my forehead.

I shake my head.

"Good." She plops onto my bed—right on my toes. It's a good thing I didn't wear my boots to bed, or they would have punctured her. And then I wonder why cowboy boots have a pointy toe, anyway? But I don't know the answer to that question.

"We need to talk about the rules of the road at the ranch," she says.

This means she's going to tell me what I can and can't

do while I'm there. Mostly what I can't do, because that's what rules are all about.

"I'm going to be working while I'm there, and Daddy's going to be taking care of Liza. I know you'll want to be in the barn, but Dad can't be because of the baby and his allergies, and JT probably won't want to be, so—"

I gasp out loud because I know what this rule of the road is going to be. "You mean I'm going to be stuck in the cabin?"

She puts her hand up to shush me. "Let me finish," she says. "The barns are pretty close to our cabin, and the staff is very nice. I think you can be out on your own a little if you and Dad use walkie-talkies to stay in touch. And you need to listen to what the ranch hands say. Got it, partner?"

"Got it."

"Don't let me down," she says.

"Mom," I say, very sweetly, "do I look like someone who would let you down?"

She kisses my forehead. "No," she says. "You don't."

After she leaves, I climb out of bed and find my boots. Real cowboys sleep with their boots on. By the middle of the night, I think real cowboys must not need much sleep. Because it is impossible to get any when you're wearing stiff, poky boots.

While we're driving to the ranch, I write a schedule of what I will do every day we're there. "Attention, everyone!" I say. "Here is what I'll be doing at the ranch."

"The suspense is killing me," says JT, closing his eyes and sighing.

"Saturday: Meet horses. Ride the one that will be mine. Sunday: Go on trail ride and eat ice cream to celebrate. Monday, Tuesday, Wednesday: Go on overnight trail ride into mountains, roast marshmallows, sing cowboy tunes, curl up with my horse and sleep under the stars."

JT opens his eyes and makes his "get real" face. "Reality check, Mary Misguided. There are no mountains around here, and cowboys don't roast marshmallows."

"How do you know?"

"I just do. That's what kids do at camp."

"Well, maybe it's what cowboys do, too," I say.

"No, it's not. They eat beef jerky. Also, horses sleep standing up."

"Don't ruin things for her, JT," says my mom.

He holds up his arms like he can't believe she's saying that. "No one thought about not ruining things for *me* when they decided to come on this dumb trip."

My mother ignores him. "What else is on your schedule, Mary Margaret?"

"As if we didn't know," JT says under his breath.

I don't let JT's bad mood anchor me down. "Thursday: Ride some more. Friday: Ridey-ride-ride!"

I don't read what's on the schedule for Saturday, which is *Hide so my family leaves without me and I can live at the ranch forever and ever.*

"Seven fun-filled days," says JT.

"Yup, all horses all the time," I say, sighing happily and shoving my list and pencil into my pocket. "Nothing but horses, horses, horses."

As soon as we get to the Lazy K Ranch, I am out of the van. Normally I would have to help unload our suitcases and bags of snacks and pillows and toys and cameras, and also the stroller, port-a-crib, bouncy seat, and CD player. But JT says if he has to listen to me talk about horses for one more second, he won't be held responsible for his actions.

"If you care about her safety, let her go," he says, once we all pile out of the van.

My dad puckers up his lips and put his finger across them. "Hmm," he says, like he's thinking about whether or not he cares about my safety. "She *is* a lot of trouble," he says. "Lil, what do you think?"

"We do need to be practical," my mom says. "If something happened to her, the baby would never get her burps out and then she'd cry and we'd all be miserable. Let's make sure nothing happens to her, shall we?"

They are serious about the burping—I'm the expert burper in our family—but I know they are kidding about everything else. My mom and dad love me all the way to Mars and sometimes all the way to Pluto. "So can I go?"

"Go!" all three of them say at the same time. "Please!"

"Thanks, JT," I say, grabbing my straw cowboy hat off the seat. I *clomp-clomp-clomp* past them in my new cowboy boots. A cloud of dust puffs up with every *clomp*, just like in the movies.

"Hold up, partner," my mom says. She digs around in Liza's diaper bag, like a dog looking for a bone, then pulls out a walkie-talkie. "Remember what we talked about. If you want to be able to run around the ranch on your own, you need to keep this with you. And look!" she says, steering the walkie-talkie toward my belt. "It even has this cute clip thing so you can wear it on your—"

I stop her hand just before it gets to my belt. "I can do it, Mom. I'm not a baby."

"Oh. Well. I was just trying to make it easy for you."

"Over and out," I say, scooting out of there.

At the barn door, I stop to mash my hat onto my head. I hook my thumbs in my pockets, just like I've seen the cowboys on TV do. Then I make my grand entrance. "HELLO, HORSES!" I say, flinging my arms open wide.

A man leading a horse out of a stall stops to look at me. "Look what the cat dragged in," he says.

"What? Where?" I look around my feet because if there's a mouse, I want to know about it. Maybe it could be my pet while I'm here.

"You, that's who," the man says. "And who might you be?"

"I might be Mary Margaret," I say, sticking out my hand to shake his. "In fact, I am." At the same time that I'm shaking his hand, I'm looking at his horse, which is very colorful. It has a white rump with brown spots and a brown neck with white spots, sort of like it couldn't decide what color it wanted to be. "That is one wild and crazy horse!"

"Terco? Nah, she's as tame as they come. Can't barely get her to move, is all."

"I've never seen a horse with freckles."

"She's an Appaloosa."

"She's the most beautiful horse I've ever seen. Can I ride her?"

He rubs her neck and she nuzzles his hand. Then he fastens the belt that keeps the saddle on. I think he didn't hear my question. "I SAID, CAN I—"

"Hold up," he says. "I heard you. I was just thinking, is all. And thinking takes time."

I scuffle my boots across the cement floor, wondering what's so hard about saying yes. Finally he says, "Kansas'll be along shortly. She can give you the test."

"You mean I can't just get on and ride? I have to take a test first?"

He snorts. "Sure you do. Can't have just any yahoo out there on the trail. Isn't good for the horses or the people. Gotta make sure people can keep their seat before we let them go on a trail ride."

"What happens if I don't pass?"

"It's not like flunking or passing. It's more like taking whatever time you need to learn what you need to know."

"Oh," I say, feeling relieved. "I'm a very fast learner. I learned to ride a bike in about an hour."

"Bikes don't weigh a thousand pounds. They don't have personalities, either," he says. "Or quirks."

"Like what kind of quirks?"

"Sometimes they're just preferences." He jerks his thumb over his shoulder. "Like Two-Bits doesn't like anybody crowding into his space. We make sure he's last in line on trail rides." He motions to the next stall down. "And that quarter horse there's name is Bob. He's afraid of hoses."

I look in at Bob, who is brown and looks shorter than the other horses. "How long before he grows into a full horse?"

"He's full growed now. Quarter horse is a breed."

"Oh, I just thought it was what you called in-between horses. I know babies are called foals and I thought quarter horse is what you called horses that are kids."

"Smart mistake," he says. "Shows you think about stuff, which is more'n I can say about most folks." He hands me the reins. "Here. You can start by leading her out to the corral."

I take a few steps in front of Terco, but she doesn't come along. I tug on the reins. "Let's go!" But Terco isn't interested in going. I tip back on the heels of my boots and pull as hard as I can. "Gid-ee-UP!" I say.

"A bitty thing like you isn't going to get a horse to do what you want, especially not Terco here. The trick is to make her *think* she wants to do it. Walk beside her like the two of you are holding hands. Sweet-talk her a little."

That's easy. I walk back to Terco, give her a nice pat on the neck. "Come on, you good little Appaloosa-poosa." She shakes her mane, which I think means "no way" in horse talk.

"You have the most glossy coat and sparkly eyes," I say.

"And, I bet that tail really flows out behind you when you run." When I tell my mom how pretty she looks, that always perks her right up. Sometimes it also changes her mind about letting me do what I want. Terco and my mom must be kind of alike that way, because after I tell her how pretty she is, Terco decides to cooperate.

"Hey, it works! Thanks . . . um, what did you say your name is again?" I secretly hope it's a real cowboy name like Shorty or Slim. He's not short and he's definitely not skinny, so neither of those work.

"Lefty," he says.

"Good! That's a good name," I say.

"I'm glad you like it," he says. "I'm kind of fond of it myself."

Terco plods along beside me as we walk to the corral. Suddenly she pricks up her ears and swings her head toward the woods that's close to the corral. A second later, I hear hooves. Pounding hooves. In another second, a horse that's as black and glistening as the oil my dad drains out of our car shoots out of the woods, running right at us. There's a rider, too, but all I see of her is a blond ponytail whipping out like a windsock. The horse skids to a stop so close that I think it's going to slide right into us. But Terco doesn't move an inch, and neither do I.

I stare up at the sweating, snorting horse. He's tossing his head and prancing in place like I do when I have to tinkle really, really bad. "That's the most beautiful horse I ever saw," I say.

"That's what you just said about Terco," Lefty says.

I think it must be hard to stay on that horse, especially because there's no saddle, but the rider doesn't notice the horse is bopping all over the place underneath her. She looks old, like she's JT's age. But she might be older. The sun makes her hair blaze like a chain of gold. She's wearing three earrings *in each ear*. Over her blue jeans, she's wearing a brown-leather-apron thingy with fringes. And she's wearing real, live spurs. She is the best girl I have ever met, even though I haven't actually met her yet. I like the friends I have, but right now it seems like they are "miniscreen" friends, like mini-DVD players. She is megascreen, like Omnimax—three stories high and surround sound. *Ka-bang!* That is the sound of me deciding Kansas and me will be friends.

"You're the best rider I've ever seen," I say.

She looks down at me like she hadn't even noticed me before. "Thanks."

"Kansas, meet Mary Margaret," says Lefty. "She came skally-hootin' into the barn a few minutes ago itching to ride."

"She'll have to wait until tomorrow. We're doing skill tests in the morning now, remember?"

All on their own, my shoulders slump because if I have to wait, it will be a heavy disappointment. I know a talking trick, though, that sometimes works. "That's okay. I've only been waiting three thousand six hundred and ninety-two days to ride a horse, so I could probably wait one more day." JT helped me figure out the math of that story problem on the way up here, before he got tired of all my horse talk.

The hard part of the talking trick is that I have to be quiet for a minute in just the right spot, which is now. After that, which is called a pause, I add, "I'm pretty sure I won't die in the middle of the night. Or lose my legs from gangrene"—I point to a spot near my ankle—"although I do have this scrape right here that could give me gangrene. You never know." I read about gangrene when we were studying the Revolutionary War at school. It's what soldiers got if they couldn't keep their wounds clean, and then the doctor would have to chop their legs off to keep the gangrene from killing them.

Lefty scratches the back of his neck while he's thinking. "I'm the one that changed the schedule," he says. "And I can just as easy make an exception to it, I guess. Kansas, whyn't you cool Twister down and then come on out."

Twister is still doing his "gotta tinkle really bad" prance. Kansas pulls back on the reins a little and Twister kind of sits back on his back two legs and spins toward the barn. Kansas leans forward and Twister takes off. She didn't even have to say anything to him.

Lefty yells, "Dadgumit! I said cool him down!" But Kansas and Twister are already gone.

The whole time I'm walking to the corral, I keep remembering Twister's shiny coat and flowing mane and tail and the way it matched Kansas's flowing ponytail. I remember the way he pranced like a parade horse, and Kansas sat so easy on him. They were a matched set.

That's the way it's going to be for me and Terco, too. We're going to gallop down the path through the woods. And everyone will stop what they are doing and say, "Man, that girl can ride, can't she?" They'll watch us as we ride off into the sunset. Terco's tail and my hair will be flying out behind us, just like Kansas's hair does. Thinking about it makes me sigh with happiness. It's going to be glorious.

"I bet Terco can spin like that," I say, when we get to the corral gate.

Lefty straightens out the blanket that's under the saddle.

I rock back and forth on my boots. "Maybe after my test, me and Terco can go riding with Kansas and Twister. Do you think so? Not right away, but pretty soon after? Do you think?"

Lefty tightens the belt that keeps the saddle on.

Then I get an even better idea. "Maybe I could take a turn on Twister."

Lefty unlatches the gate to the corral and we go in. It seems like Lefty has forgotten how to talk. "Do you think I could sometime? Remember how I said I am a fast learner?"

Finally he says, "There's a reason that horse is called Twister. When conditions are right, he'll uproot everything in his path and likely take the horns off the devil."

"Oh-ho-ho," I say, because my dad is a big jokester, too,

and I know when someone is kidding around. "Nobody's that mean. He probably just has a lot of spunk."

"Yes, ma'am, he does. And he needs a lot of help reining it in. Kansas handles him easy, but that's because she was practically born on a horse. If you weren't born with horse sense, then you gotta go out and get it if you want to ride a horse like Twister."

I would've been born on a horse, except my family was living in the city when I was born, and horses aren't allowed in the city. So I missed that chance. Fortunately, I was born with an extra sense besides the five normal senses. And that extra sense is horse sense. Which means I will be a natural at this.

3. Giddyup!

Y ou ain't scared of horses, are you?" Lefty asks.

"No. I think they are the kindest, gentlest giants in the animal kingdom."

"Good, because horses know when you're scared. They'll use it against you."

Over Lefty's shoulder I see JT coming up to the corral. "Hi, JT," I say, waving wildly to make sure he sees me. "Are you coming out to ride?" He shakes his head. "Do you want to watch me?"

He climbs up onto a post that's outside the corral. "If you can do it without talking about it," he says.

I jerk my thumb toward Lefty, which I now know is the way cowboys point. "This is Lefty," I say. "Kansas is coming in a minute to see how good I ride. Wait till you meet her. She's great and a really good rider."

But then a thought whams into my brain like an ice ball: I don't want to share Kansas with JT. She and I are on our way to being friends and I don't want him squeezing between us, doing weird teenage stuff and distracting her away from me. So I add, "But she's too old for you."

JT makes a face so that I'll think he doesn't care.

I look down just in time to sidestep a big pile of horse you-know-what—I don't want any of *that* on my red boots—and then brush the tops of them off with my hand so they still look new.

"You might have to choose between learning to ride and keeping your boots clear of dung," Lefty says, watching me.

"I'm pretty sure I can do both. I learned how to do two things at once from my mom."

"Anybody tell you about the Rider Show-Off on Friday? It's to give guests a chance to show off what they've learned."

"Can me and Terco be in it?"

"Sure," he says. "You and anybody else staying here."

"Are there ribbons and trophies?"

He nods. "Riders just do simple things. Walking a horse through an obstacle course. Racing down to the other end of the corral to get a flag. But folks seem to have a good time."

I dig into my pocket and pull out my pencil and list of things I'm going to do. I add *Win trophy* next to Friday.

"Maybe you should add 'Build self-confidence' to that list," Lefty says.

"No, I'm pretty good on confidence already," I say. "My mom says I came out this way."

"Is that right?"

"Yup. That's what she says. So, anyway, which nights do you do overnight trail rides?"

"We don't at this time of year. It's still too cold and muddy."

I take a deep breath. "Wait. Let me get this head-on. First, I have to take a test. Second, I don't get to sleep out under the stars with my horse."

"That's right."

I sigh and scratch *Go on overnight trail ride into mountains, roast marshmallows, sing cowboy tunes, curl up with my horse and sleep under the stars* off my list. Then I shove it back into my pocket. This is not going like it's supposed to, exactly. Still, it's hard to be down when there's a real, live, breathing horse with freckles standing right next to me.

While we wait for Kansas I smooth Terco's mane down, but it pops right back up again. It's like her mane is one long cowlick. Terco hangs her nose to the ground and closes her eyes. I hop around swatting at the flies as soon as they land anywhere on her spotty body. I flick at one a couple of times before I realize that it's a dot and not a fly. "Ooops! Sorry," I whisper to Terco.

The night before we came to the ranch, JT found a list of cowboy words on the Internet and printed them out for me. Now I know them all—*dogies* (cows), *chuck* (food), *chuck wagon* (where you get the chuck), and *knot head* (dummy)—so I can talk just like a cowboy. Which I plan to.

So when Kansas comes up, I say, "Howdy!"

She rolls her eyes. "Hi."

Lefty claps her on the back. "Don't be ornery with the guests," he says. Then he says to me, "Listen to what she's saying instead of how she's saying it and you'll learn plenty."

After he leaves, she puts one hand on her hip and says, "I can already see about three things you're doing wrong just standin' there."

All I'm doing is standing in front of Terco, petting her soft nose, which is my favorite thing to do with horses. I look at Terco and at my boots and at the reins in my hand. As far as I can tell, I'm doing everything right. "Like what?"

"First off, don't ever stand square in front of a horse. See this?" she says, pointing to Terco's half-open eye.

"Yeah, it's an eye."

"But look at where it's at—on the side of her head. Horses can't see you if you stand dead-on in front of them. So that's the first thing. Stand beside the horse."

I move over to Terco's right side.

"See, that's wrong, too. You're supposed to stand on the horse's left side. Left is right."

"Why?"

"Why what?"

"Why is left right?"

"It just is, is all."

"Well, who decided it?"

"It doesn't matter. That's just the way it is." She is starting to sound annoyed. Ever since he turned thirteen, JT gets annoyed a lot, so I know what annoyed sounds like.

"Then why can't right be right?" I ask. "That makes more sense, and it's easier to remember."

"Because the horses know that left is right."

"All horses? As soon as they are born?"

"Yes! No! I mean—"

She looks around like she can't believe what she's hearing. When she sees JT, she points to me and says, "Are you related to her?"

"Sadly, yes," JT says.

"Is she always like this?"

He nods.

"Is there a trick to shutting her up?"

"Throwing information at her sometimes works. I could get the answer to her question online if you have a computer with Internet access."

"The ranch doesn't have that."

"Well, maybe you could do it from home," JT says.

"We don't have a computer at home."

"You don't have a computer?" This is a shocker to me. I thought all houses came with computers, just like they come with ovens and toilets.

"No," she snips. "We don't. Not everyone is like you."

"No big deal," JT says.

"Oh, ha ha! It is, too," I say, because that is a big joke. JT can't live without a computer. "If we didn't have a computer, you'd—"

"Let it go, Mary Margaret," he says, in his "trust me this is important" voice. "Left is right."

Sometimes, I hate having a big brother. It's like he's a giant poster that says to me and everyone else, I'M **BIG**! MARY MARGARET IS small.

"GRRR-ruff!" I bark, to let him know that I am mad. I don't say anything more about the computer, but it's only because I don't want to ruin my chances to get on a horse. I want to get on Terco so I can pass the test. Because once I pass the test, I can do like I planned and ride horses whenever I want. And that will be sheer and utter happiness.

I scoot over to Terco's left side. I see another fly on her rump and I fling myself at it with my arms open wide.

"Whoa, whoa, whoa," Kansas says. "Horses spook easily. You gotta move real slow. You think you can do that, Princess?"

All I want is for Kansas to like me and to be good at riding. (Someday I'd also like to have a horse and a dog and maybe play hockey, but I mean *right then* all I want is for Kansas to like me and to be good at riding.) But it seems like neither of those things is going so well right then. So when she asks me if I think I can do that, I swallow hard and nod. And even though I don't like the name Princess, I think that Kansas giving me a nickname is a good thing. All cowboys have nicknames. So I let that go, too.

"What are the other two things I was doing wrong?" I ask.

She flips her ponytail so it's behind her back. "Forget

those for now," she says. "You can't learn everything at once. Let's just get you on Terco." She folds her hands together and turns them upside down. "Put one hand on my shoulder and your knee in my hands and I'll give you a leg up."

"Wait a minute," I say. I reach down and carefully tuck the tassels into each of my boots. "Don't want them to get dirty."

"Whenever you're ready, Princess," she says.

"I'm ready." When I put my hand on her shoulder, I can smell her hair. It smells like strawberries. I stick my tongue out to lick it, just to see if it tastes as good as it smells. Right then she looks up. "What are you doing?" she asks.

"Nothing," I say.

"You were going to lick my head!"

"Your hair—it smelled like strawberries," I say, trying to explain.

"So what?" she says. "It's my hair and you don't get to lick it!"

I don't know why she's so mad. "I'm sorry. I just liked it, is all."

She sighs and says, "We can try this again on the condition that you keep your tongue to yourself. Do you swear to it?"

We're not allowed to swear in our house, so I just nod. I clamp my teeth together to make sure my tongue doesn't hang out accidentally. She cups her hands together to make a stirrup again. I put my knee into them. Just as she starts to lift me, my walkie-talkie crackles and my dad's voice says, "Report in, Wrangler Anderson. Over." Kansas drops my knee and jumps back.

"Smokin' frijoles," she said. "You want to give poor Terco a heart attack? Shut that thing off."

"I can't," I say. "My mom says I need to keep it with me if I want to be on my own." I press the talk button and say, "I'm in the corral with a wrangler. Getting on a horse!"

"Roger that," my dad says. "There's a horse over here wearing just socks."

"*What?* Over."

"Apparently he lost his shoes. Over."

I start to giggle but stop myself when I see Kansas roll her eyes. "Da-ad," I say. "Over."

"Sorry. Couldn't help myself. If JT is there, send him to the cabin. Over."

"Okay. Over."

"Roger that. Over and out."

"Over and out," I say. Then I tell JT to leave me and Kansas alone and to get on back to the cabin. Only I say it a little nicer than that.

"I suppose you have to be home in time for dinner, too," Kansas says.

"Well, yeah. Don't you?"

"Nah. I cook for myself when I get home—if I get home. Sometimes I just sleep here. Nobody's mollycoddled me since I've been six."

"What happened then?"

"I grew up, is all." She does that stirrup thing with her hands again and lifts me up enough so I can swing my other leg over the saddle, and then suddenly I'm sitting exactly where I'm supposed to be—high on a horse. "To make her turn left, lay the reins against the right side of her neck, like this," Kansas says, showing me how. "To make her turn right, lay the reins against the left side. To make her stop—"

"I know. Pull back and say *whoaaaa*."

"Right, but also lean back in the saddle. You want me to walk around the corral with you until you get the hang of it?"

"No, I can do it." I know Terco's a good girl. I know she'll do whatever I ask her to. Because that's the way it is between a horse and rider when they understand each other. It's like they share a brain.

Except Terco's half of the brain is taking a nap right now. "*Zcht, zcht!*" I cluck. Terco twitches her ears. "*ZCHT, ZCHT!*" I cluck again.

"Give her some boot," Kansas says. "You know—kick her."

"What if I hurt her?"

Kansas laughs. "Impossible. The kick just shows her you're serious. You have to show her who's boss."

"Come on, Terco," I say, rubbing my heels against her belly. "You and me are a team. You have to help me pass this test so we can go riding on the trail. You'd like that, wouldn't you, to go riding on the trail?"

Terco waggles a fly off her head. I give her a little kick but she still doesn't move.

Kansas stands with her legs far apart and her hands in her back pockets. "I'm telling you, sissy kicks won't work with Terco."

"You just don't understand her. Lefty said to sweet-talk her and it worked."

"It worked because Terco knows Lefty means business."

I lean over and hug Terco's neck. "Come on," I say to Terco. "Giddyup now so I won't have to kick you." I talk sweet to her for as long as I can think up sweet words to say, which is a long time because I really like horses. Terco doesn't move an inch. In fact, it looks like all my sweet talk put her to sleep.

Finally I get mad and I have to talk sour instead of sweet to her. "I have cowboy boots and I'm not afraid to use them," I growl at her. "So MOVE YOUR BIG, FRECKLY *BUTT*!" I am not allowed to say that word at our house, but I'm not at our house or even our cabin, and it feels good to roar it out. I grab the saddle horn tight so I can be ready for anything Terco does. I lift my legs out as far as I can and bring them down as hard as I can. Terco twitches her ears like she's thinking about what I said. Then she takes a step, and another, and another.

"Great! You got her to plod," Kansas says, clapping. "Now keep her going."

I am so happy right then, because I did it. I got her to go! And Kansas said it was great that I did. So we are definitely on our way to being good friends, probably.

Everything looks different from on top of Terco. The ranch is bigger. I feel like *I'm* bigger. And I'm definitely taller. I can see all the way over to the cabins, where Liza's stroller is parked under a tree. My dad is sitting next to it. "Hey, Dad," I yell, standing up in my stirrups and waving my arm around like a windmill. "Look at me! I'm riding!" But he's too far away and doesn't hear me.

"Cut it out. You're going to spook the horse," says Kansas.

I look down at Terco, who is still just plodding along. "Terco's not spooked," I say.

"The joke around here is that Terco's barely *alive,*" Kansas says. "We like to say that horse is dead, she just won't lay down. But not all horses are like Terco."

Now that I have got Terco going, horseback riding is just as easy as I thought it was going to be. I am a great rider, because here I am, up on a horse, riding around the corral on my very first try without even falling off. But then after just one time walking around the corral, Terco gets to the gate and stops.

"Don't let her do that," Kansas says. "Did you ask her to do that?"

"No."

"Then don't you let her. She's thinking she's in control. Show her she's not! Make her keep going."

I talk sweet to her. I lay the reins on her neck just like Kansas showed me. I kick her again and again. My mind is made up that she is going to go around the corral again. But her mind is made up that she's not.

Kansas keeps shouting at me to make her go, even though that's what I'm already trying to do. I don't know why she has to be so mean about it, but it makes me feel mean, too. I yell at Terco. "It's going to be all your fault if we don't ever get out of this corral! Don't you care?"

Terco waggles her head.

And Kansas says I'm stuck in the kiddie corral for at least another day.

here's nothing to do here," JT says on Monday morning. He tosses a brochure about the ranch onto the coffee table. "No wireless Internet access, not even a computer to check e-mail with—at least not that I could find."

"Nothing to do?" I say. "Why, you're as crazy as popcorn on a hot stove!" Lefty said that about Twister yesterday and I've been waiting for a chance to use it. I thought JT would like it, but he just scowls.

I try to change his mind. "There's riding and a petting corral and horseshoes and did you see Goose?" Goose is a baby goat who wears a red bandanna and runs around free all over the ranch. Mostly he follows Kansas around like she's his mom. That's because Kansas took care of Goose when his real mom found out she didn't like being a mom and she quit that job.

"That's another thing—all the dumb names," JT says. He sits down on the cabin floor and starts doing stretches. He's on the cross-country team at school and is already pretty good at it even though this is his first year. "A goat that's named Goose. Why don't they give it a normal goat name?"

My dad looks up from burping Liza. "Such as . . . ?" I hope Liza belts out a big one soon, otherwise the expert Liza-Burper is going to have to do it. In other words, me.

"I don't know. Billy? Something that makes sense."

"But Goose does make sense. Kansas says he got his name because he gooses everyone—you know, pokes at them with his nose in their . . ." and I stick out my behind and point to it. Kansas told me so last night when she was putting Terco away and Goose was trailing around after her, the way toilet paper does when it gets stuck to the bottom of your shoe.

My dad passes Liza over to me, smiling like he gets it, but JT isn't listening. "Even the furniture is annoying," JT says. "Hooks in the bathrooms made out of bent horseshoes and bar stools with seats made out of old saddles so you have to straddle them. They aren't even comfortable."

"Ohhh, I love those things," I say with a sigh, thinking about the polished leather and the way the bar stool creaks when I settle into it. I almost forget that I'm rubbing Liza's back instead of one of those saddle stools. "I wish we had some of those."

"You would," he says.

"*Ble-UURP!*" goes Liza.

"Kansas said that every one of those saddles has something behind it."

"Yeah, a *horse's* behind," he says.

"She meant each saddle has a *story* behind it," I say.

"I'm getting the message loud and clear that you don't want to be here," my dad says to JT. "Maybe if you tried to have a good time, you would."

"I've been trying for two whole days," JT says. "It's impossible."

"No, it's not," I say. "I've flunked the riding test twice and I'm having a good time."

"Stay out of it," JT says.

I shrug. "I'm just trying to be helpful and you said it was impossible but *impossible* means it's not possible and since I am having a good time then it *is* possible and—"

"Mary Margaret," my dad says, and he shakes his head at me. Which means I should zip up my lips. So I do. He turns back to JT. "It's time to reach into the bag for a new attitude."

JT lies down on the floor and stretches his body into an L. I can't walk around him because his legs and arms are all over the place. To get Liza back to my dad I have to hop over an arm and two legs. When I get to the second leg, Liza spits up right on JT's thigh. He makes a face and says, "I didn't pack any other attitudes."

My dad picks up JT's stinky running shoes and drops them right next to JT's head. "Then go find one. Go ask Mom if she needs help with something. Or go running. Or read a book. Just do something."

I don't get why JT doesn't like it here. He must just

need some help seeing how great it is. "You could come with me to the barn," I say. "And watch me ride. I'm pretty sure that today *finally* I'll get out of the kiddie corral, if Terco cooperates." She listened a little more to me yesterday, so I have high hopes.

"No thanks," he says, reaching for his shoes. "I'm going for a run. I need to get out of here."

"That's one thing you can do here. Kansas said—"

But JT gets out of there before I can even finish that sentence. I guess he doesn't care what Kansas says, which is hard to believe when you're me.

I wander into the bedroom, which my mom is also using as her office—"Party Central" she calls it—and ask her what she's doing.

"Obsessing. Obsessing about everything that could go wrong for the party."

"But you're good at your job so you won't let anything go wrong."

My mom groans. "Oh, Loverly. There are so many things that could go wrong. The chef could throw a temper tantrum—you can't believe how often that happens! Or the magician I've hired might not show up at the last minute. Or it could rain!"

"Yeah," I say. I stand with my legs far apart and my hands in my back pockets, the way Kansas does.

My mom lifts an eyebrow at me. "That's not a very ladylike way to stand."

"It's comfortable," I say, staggering a few steps to keep

myself from falling over. I change the subject. "It looks like it might rain today."

"Better today than on Wednesday for the party," she says.

I watch her put little gold earrings in her ears. I can't wait until I can wear earrings. I used to think I'd wear bright dangly ones, the kind that people stare at. But now I know that I'll wear ones just like the ones Kansas wears—silver horseshoes, hoops, and tiny emeralds.

"Could the magician cast a spell on someone—like me, or a horse?"

"He's not that kind of magician. He does card tricks, not spells. And they'd better be good."

"Oh," I say, feeling disappointed. "I was hoping he could help me and Terco go on a trail ride."

"Lucky you have a mother," she says. She walks over and pulls one of my hands out of my back pocket so she can look at my palm. "Because mothers have special powers and see a little bit about the future." She closes her eyes and sways back and forth. "Mary Mar-gar-et," she says in a spooky voice. "I can see that yes—yes, you will go on a trail ride . . . if you keep practicing." She opens her eyes and smiles at me.

"I know you're kidding. If you really had special powers, then I'd be able to do it without practicing."

She drops my hand. "Well, there's only so much a mother can do—even a mother with special powers. I'm sorry there aren't more kids here for you to play with. I guess not many other schools are on spring break this week."

"It's okay. I like hanging out with Terco and Goose and Lefty. And Kansas. Even though she's kind of prickly. All I was going to do was lick her hair. I don't know why she got so excitable about it. And JT says I offended her because I acted like it was a crime she didn't have a computer. But I was just surprised."

"It sounds like you two got off on the wrong foot," she says.

"And she stayed there," I say. "Yesterday was a lot like the day before. Kansas told me what to do. Then I told Terco what to do. Then Terco wouldn't do it! And Kansas acted like it was my fault. So I don't know how to get her off the wrong foot."

My mom nods like she understands and pulls me into her so she can hug me. "Sometimes it's hard."

"Mom?" I say, into her arm. "What's it like to be in love?"

"Well, you like the other person a lot and want to spend all your time with him. Why?"

"I think I might be in love with Kansas."

She squeezes me tighter. "Oh yes. A girl crush. I had one on my piano teacher when I was about your age. I remember taking her a bunch of daisies for her birthday and writing her a poem."

"What happened?"

My mom laughs. "Right before I was going to give

them to her, her boyfriend showed up with a diamond ring and proposed to her. My daisies didn't have much of an impact, I'm afraid."

"I like daisies better."

She laughs again and squeezes me even tighter.

"Mom?" I say.

"Yes?"

"I can't breathe."

She unwraps her arms. "Sorry, Loverly. Listen, I know you like Kansas and want her to like you. Just be yourself and give her the chance to get to know you better."

I would give Kansas the chance—if only I could find her! It seems like every time I go to the barn, she has just left there and the other wranglers never know where she went. I check in the toolshed, the corral, the chuck wagon, and even the honey shed, which is what they call the place where all the horse poo—I mean *dung*—gets dumped before it gets spread on the fields.

Every time I ask if anyone knows where Kansas is, I get, "She was here a minute ago." Or "Couldn't tell ya." And whenever I do find Kansas and tell her how hard she is to find, she always says, "There's a reason for that," which I think must be her way of saying she's busy.

My mom tells me that I am determined, which means I know what I want. My dad says I'm resourceful, which means I find a way to get what I want. It's a good thing that I am both or I might never find Kansas. And if I can't ever find her, then how can she get to know me better so we can get to be friends?

Fortunately, I have an idea. All I have to do is listen for Goose. When I hear Goose bleating from the barn, I trot right over there. Wherever Goose is, that's where Kansas will be! I sneak in real quiet so I can surprise her.

"Hi! It's me, your favorite wrangler," I say.

"Oh, hey," she says. She doesn't sound very excited but that's probably just because she's working.

Wrangler Brett comes out of a stall and tips his hat at me as he walks by. That's the thing about a lot of these wranglers. They are nice but they don't talk very much. I do talk, so they are probably glad to have me around to fill up the long spaces of quiet between when one wrangler says "yup" and the next one says "nope."

I climb onto a stack of hay and settle in for a chat. "What are you doing?"

"What does it look like?" She scoops up some grain from the sack that's in a wheelbarrow and dumps it into a bin in the stall, using one elbow to keep Goose away from the grain.

"That's easy. Putting grain into the bowls in each stall." I notice there's a layer of dust on my boots, so I lean over and spit on them—*pittuth*. Then I polish my boots with the bottom of my shirt until they shine.

She pushes the wheelbarrow to the next stall and does the same thing. Goose trots behind her, bumping her leg with his head.

"How do you know how much each horse gets?"

"By size. Horses get two scoops. Ponies, just one."

"I'm amounded by how much you know about horses."

Kansas looks at me like she's trying to figure out if I'm kidding her. "It's not brain surgery. Besides, don't you mean astounded?"

"No. Amazed plus astounded. I'm amounded. Why are you feeding them now?"

She sighs. "So the horses don't mind coming to work."

"Oh, like my mom needs her coffee in the morning to get going. Before she gets her first cup, she's crabby! Ask her a question and all she'll do is grunt because she just doesn't want to talk or even think before she has her coffee. Know what I mean?"

Kansas grunts.

I guess she's not very interested in coffee, so I change the subject. "I have a pet rabbit at home."

"You have a rodent for a pet?"

I know for real and for true that rabbits are not rodents, and I'm dying to tell her so. But I bet she wouldn't like being wrong and I don't want to ruin our friendship when it's just getting going. So I just say, "Her name is Hershey, and she's brown and white. She comes when I make kissing sounds. Like this." I put my lips together and go *pwip, pwip, pwip*. "Does Twister do that?"

She wipes her hands on her jeans. "Nope."

"Want me to teach him how?" I ask.

Wrangler Brett walks by. His head is down and his hat

is hiding most of his face, but I think he's grinning a little.

"Nope," Kansas says. "He comes when I whistle. I guess that's good enough."

"But the kissing sounds are great because it's like a secret signal between you. See, nobody would know that you'd be calling him. That worked really well once when me and Hershey were in a play."

"Twister and I don't do plays," she says.

"Well, if you ever change your mind . . ."

Kansas grunts and goes to the next stall. I stick my legs straight out and clunk my boots together, just because I like the noise they make when the heels hit each other. It's like a new way to clap—a cowboy way to clap. And I feel like clapping because Kansas is getting to know me now, and we had that nice little talk, and I think that now we're getting off on the right foot. Even Wrangler Brett can see that.

My walkie-talkie crackles and my dad's voice says, "Location check, over."

"Barn. Over."

"Roger," he says. "Over and out."

"I don't see how you can stand to be hobbled by that thing," Kansas says from the stall.

"What do you mean, hobbled?"

"Hobbling's what cowboys do with their horses when they are out on the range and don't have a barn or pasture to put them in." She comes out and wheels the wheelbarrow to the next stall. "They tie a rope, but kind of loose, around all four legs. That way the horse can move, but not very far."

I look at the walkie-talkie. I never thought of it like that before. "Oh," I say.

"How old did you say you are?"

"Nine."

She shrugs. "I guess ranch kids grow up faster than city kids. By the time you're nine, there's lots of stuff you have to do on your own—chores and responsibilities."

"I have chores and responsibilities, too!" I say, all excited because Kansas and me have something in common. "I set the table and feed Hershey and burp my little sister Liza."

"You ever hauled water? Or cleaned out stalls all day? Or helped dig a grave for a calf that died?"

"No."

"Those are what I'm talking about. Real chores."

It's true that her chores are bigger and harder. But it's not my fault that my family lives in town, where nobody needs to haul water and where large animals can't live. And if they can't live there, they can't die there, so I'll never be able to bury a dead one, even if I wanted to. "I'd do those chores if I had the chance," I say.

"You have the chance now."

I look at Kansas's boots, which are so dirty that I can't tell what color they are. They might be brown, or they might just look brown because of what's on them. "No thanks," I say. Because my new clean red boots make me very happy and I want to keep them clean and red.

"That's what I thought," she says.

"Where do all the horses go while you do this?"

"The pasture. That's where they stay at night."

"Aren't you worried about hustlers stealing them?"

"You mean *rustler*. A hustler is a cheat."

"Anybody who steals a horse *is* a cheat," I say. "*Hustler*'s a better word for it than *rustler*, because you have to hustle the horse you stole right out of there before you get caught." I am feeling friendly so I add, "But *rustler* works, too. So are you scared of them?"

She snorts like a horse. "No-ho."

"Why not?"

"Because there aren't any, that's why."

"Well, where'd they all go? What happened to them?"

"I don't know." She puts grain into the last stall. "You done, Brett?"

"Yup," he says.

"Okay, Joe. Open the gate," she yells. She points at me. "You stay there, unless you want to get trampled."

Before I can ask why, the barn hallway is full of horses. Terco turns left into the stall that says TERCO and Two-Bits turns right into the stall that says TWO-BITS and Bob goes into the BOB stall beside Two-Bits' stall.

"Hey, they can read," I say. Kansas gives me a look. I think it's a "don't be a knot head" look. I slump a little. "Well, I know they really can't, but how do they know which stall is theirs?"

Kansas shrugs. "Habit. If one of them goes into the wrong one, it throws them all off."

I nod and we watch all the other horses find their stalls. It feels friendly there with me and Kansas watching the rest of the horses coming home, which is how I think of it.

Being all quiet like that is nice, for about a minute. After that my mouth gets ants in its pants. "So, just guess," I say.

Goose squeezes around Kansas and starts eating grain from the wheelbarrow. She pushes him away. "Huh? What do you mean, just guess?"

"Guess what happened to all the rustlers. I know there used to be some. I read about them in books."

"I don't feel like it."

"Come on! Just guess."

Wrangler Brett is zigzagging in and out of stalls, clipping each horse's halter to the lead rope. Kansas picks up a grooming kit and starts brushing Two-Bits, who is in the closest stall. "They moved to North Dakota and opened a restaurant that serves breakfast all day, and at night they all go to ballet class."

"They do not!" I say.

"You wanted me to guess, so I guessed."

"Yeah, but that's not a serious guess. Do a serious guess, like they all ended up in Alcatraz or they all died in a shoot-out."

Kansas rests her forehead against Two-Bits' rump and

covers her head with both of her arms. When she lifts her head up again, she says, "If I guess, will you stop all that yipping?"

"You want me to stop talking?"

"YES!"

"But if I don't talk, who will? There wouldn't be anything but quiet."

"Right!" she says, putting the accent on the *T*.

"But . . . I always talk," I say. "I'm a natural at it."

"Then find someone else to talk to! Criminy! You're worse than Goose, always wanting to follow me around, bugging me while I work."

Brett zigs out of a stall. "Careful with them spurs," he mutters to Kansas.

"I'm trying," she says. "But it's like she can't *not* talk."

That punctures my heart a little, because all I'm doing is being myself, like my mom said I should. But being myself is not making Kansas like me. I quick poke my finger onto my chest right above my heart, where it feels like the hole is, so that all my feelings won't spill out of me.

"I can too not talk," I say. "And for your information, you are out-of-date about rabbits. A long time ago somebody important gave rabbits and hares their own category, so they aren't rodents." Since my mouth is already moving, all on its own it adds, "Which you would know if you had a computer." Then I clomp my punctured heart right out of there.

· · ·

Lefty is in the garage, leaning over a quad, which looks like a motorcycle except it has four wheels. The wranglers use it to get somewhere quick when they don't have a horse. Lefty is looking down at something on the quad, so I'm surprised when he says, "Hi, Mary Margaret."

My plan is to not say anything, just to prove that I can too not talk, but that plan lasts about a minute and then I forget about it. "How'd you know it was me?"

"Sound of your boots. How's it going? You learning what you need to win the Rider Show-Off trophy?"

"Um, yeah," I say. "I know how to walk, so that's a start, and I know there'll be barrels in the ring, so I've checked those out. You know, I've walked around them and stuff."

My voice doesn't have any zip, though, and that's probably how Lefty knows I don't want to trophy-talk right then. He looks up at me and sees my finger that's poked into my chest over my heart. "Something wrong?" he asks.

"Not really," I say. But I keep my finger right where it's at.

"Then hand me that little wrench," he says, pointing to a tool on the rack attached to the seat. I give it to him and he goes back to work. "Dadgum kids," he grumbles. "Riding this thing into the ground like it's a toy instead of a piece of machinery."

I walk around to the other side of the quad so I can climb onto the seat without getting into Lefty's way. After a few minutes of sitting on the quad, I forget all about the hole in me. I start touching all the buttons and knobs, which I'm sure is okay because the quad is not on, which means it's not dangerous. Or even alive. "What do the silver handles do?"

"Those are the brakes."

"Oh, like on my bike." I play with a little black knobby thing. "What about this?"

"That's how you make it go."

"Does Kansas drive this?"

"Not until she's sixteen, she doesn't. Nobody under sixteen drives it. It's against the law."

I see the key but before I can even start to move my hand that way, Lefty says, "Don't touch the key!"

So I lie all the way back on the seat and reach one hand behind me. I pick up the tools one at a time and say what each one is, as I hold it straight up over my head. "Screwdriver. Hammer. Skinny silver thingy. Giant wrench. And I already gave you the baby wrench."

"The baby's a spark-plug wrench," he says, "which is what I'm fixin'."

"What's a spark plug?"

Kansas walks in, with Goose right behind her, and shoves stuff around on the shelf like she's looking for something.

"Spark plugs get the engine going, leastwise when they're connected righ—"

Kansas knocks an empty paint can off the shelf and it bounces across the cement floor—*clankity*-CLANK, *clankity*-CLANK-*clank-clank*—and almost hits Goose, who sniffs at it. Kansas shrugs when Lefty looks at her.

"Wranglers ride it hard and then wonder why it quits 'em."

Kansas slides something metal across the metal shelf. *Screech! Scree-eech!*

Lefty stops talking to me and says to Kansas, "Can you hush your hands up over there? With all that racket you're making, I can't even think, let alone talk to Mary Margaret."

"Why bother?" she says, picking up a can. "Nothing sticks. There's a chute that goes clean through from her ears to her mouth and it's waxed and polished. Telling her anything is a waste of time."

"If you can't be civil, then *git*," Lefty says to her.

Kansas throws a dirty look at me. Before I remember that my finger isn't in that hole near my heart, most of the rest of me trickles out. I guess all my words do, too, because even though my mouth is open, nothing comes out.

5. Baby, I'm Blue

After Kansas *gits*, and Goose, too, I watch Lefty put his tools away. Neither of us says anything. In the big double sink, he washes his hands, all the way up to his elbows. He holds the soap out to me. "Wash up," he says. "I could use your help with something."

I take the soap and do what he says because I don't have anything better to do. We walk together to a shed that's close to the corral. It's a little dark inside and it smells musty, like my grandpa's old barn, but sweet, too, like a sweaty horse. There's only one stall in the shed, but it's a big one.

"Hey, Blue," Lefty says in a low voice to the horse inside. "What you got for us this time?"

Blue is standing with her rump to the stall door, but she turns her head to look at Lefty. A brown baby horse, freshly born, is lying beside her. The baby's hair is still damp.

"Another filly," he says. "Good work."

When the baby sees us, she scrabbles her legs around.

She pushes up with her front legs stuck out straight in front of her, like furry toothpicks, until she's sitting on her rump. Then she kind of heaves around, trying to stand up, except her back legs won't cooperate. She finally gets part-way up but her front legs bend like she's too heavy for them. Then she gets all the way up, and her front legs stop working and she falls down again.

"What's wrong with her?" I ask.

"Nothin'," says Lefty. "It's what newborn horses do."

The baby's mother watches but doesn't do anything. The baby raises her head and braces her front legs again. Her back legs scramble around under her for a minute, then she stops and lays her head down, like she's all done being determined.

"She's giving up!"

Lefty shakes his head. "Not in her nature to give up."

"Can't we help her?"

"Helping her now would be hurting her. Struggling makes her legs stronger. And every time she falls, she learns something new about how not to." He crosses his arms and leans on the edge of the stall. "You watch. In a few minutes, she'll be steady enough. In an hour, she'll be trying to run. In two hours, she'll be running circles around her mom."

We watch until the filly has figured out how to work her legs and isn't so wobbly anymore. Lefty slides open the stall door. "Move real slow," he says. "Let Baby Blue smell you good and then just rub her slowly all over her body."

"What about Blue, though?" I ask, because every time we take a step, so do Blue's hind legs, so that her rump is always between us and her baby.

"She's an old pro," says Lefty. "She knows the routine. She's just a little nervous because she doesn't know you. I'll worry about her. You just make nice with Baby Blue."

So I do. I rub her fuzzy neck and shoulders. I run my hand down her stubby mane, across her back, and over her skinny rump. I kiss her nose, and it is the softest horse nose I have ever kissed. Lefty says if I blow my breath up her nostril, she'll remember me forever. So I do.

Mostly Baby Blue lets me do all of it, except when I hop up and down with excitement because this is a dream come true. But then Lefty just reminds me and I slow down again. And after a while, I can hug her neck and bury my face in her mane, and she nuzzles me like we have been best friends for our whole lives.

My heart goes *zing!*

All of me that poured out before somehow gets sucked right back up into me through the same hole that Kansas made when she was mean. And all my words come back, too, so I line a few of them up into a poem.

> *Baby Blue,*
> *My love is so true.*
> *Who needs a pup?*
> *You filly me up!*

When it's time to go, Lefty says, "You know what you just did?"

"I made a friend."

Lefty nods. "You also just taught Baby Blue that people will never hurt her."

Helping Baby Blue makes me feel warm from the inside out, like there's a sun shining not on my chest but *in* my chest. And I'm glad for Baby Blue that nobody will hurt her. Probably nobody will ever even hurt her feelings. Which would be nice.

Over the walkie-talkie, my dad tells me he needs me back at the cabin. Before I go, I tell Lefty thanks. "Spending time with Baby Blue made me feel good. She's special."

"They all are," he says.

On my way back to the cabin, I stop by the big barn to give Terco a carrot. Twister is hanging his head out of his stall, so I give him one, too. Then I blow my breath up his nose. He might not remember me forever, but maybe he'll at least remember me while I'm here at the ranch.

Wrangler Brett, carrying a bucket of tools, stops beside me. At first he doesn't say anything, so I start right in. "Twister and me are—"

But Brett holds up his hand to stop me. Looking in at Twister, he says, "I got something to say."

I shrug. "Okay."

"What I want to say is, don't take it personal—what Kansas says. She'll come around."

"How?"

"With her, you never know what bee is in her bonnet, or how to get it out. Sometimes I think all she needs is a good laugh to loosen her up." He turns to leave. "But it's not your burden and you shouldn't have to bear it."

"Okay," I say, even though I don't understand everything he said. "Thanks."

I walk past the game room just as JT is coming out. I don't feel like talking, but JT does. He must be as bored as he says he is. "Hey, Mary Mosey-on-Down," he says.

"Hi."

"Just hi? That's it? No 'Kansas said this or Kansas said that'? No 'JT come watch me jounce around on a horse'"?

"No."

"How about a catchy cowboy phrase? You must be able to come up with one of those."

I can remember only one. "If you didn't have such a puny thinker, you could come up with your own," I say.

"Puny thinker?!" JT pretends that he's all shocked and that gives me a twitchy smile, even though I am not in the mood to smile.

"Cut it out," I say. "I want to be alone because I have stuff to figure out."

He shoves his hands into the pockets in his blue jeans. "Maybe I could help. Even a puny thinker is better than none. What's going on?"

"I am never going to pass that stupid riding test."

"Sure you will. You're getting better all the time."

"First, it's not me that has to get better. I'm already good. It's Terco that has to get better."

"Right. *Terco's* fault. I forgot about that."

"I'm not going to pass because Kansas doesn't like me."

"What did you do this time?"

"Nothing! I was just being myself! She said I talk too much."

JT pretends he's all shocked again. *"You?"* he says. *"Talk too much?"*

I sock him in the arm, but not hard.

"And?" he says. JT knows there is usually more to my stories than I tell right away.

"And she thought rabbits were rodents, and I told her she's wrong and that she'd know that if she had a computer."

JT cuffs me across the head, but not hard. "Didn't you remember that's a sore spot of hers?"

"Yes, I remembered," I say. "That's why I did it!"

"And you wonder why she doesn't like you."

"Well, calling Hershey a rodent is a sore spot with *me*," I say. "So she had it coming."

"So you think it might help to . . ." JT waves his hands toward himself, like I'm supposed to say the next word. I don't say anything. He tries again. "When you've said something dumb to someone, you can go to the person and say, 'I'm . . .'"

I still don't say anything.

"Starts with an *s* . . ." He puts one hand in front of the other like he's pulling on a rope, like he's trying to pull the word out of me.

I zip my lip up tight. I know the word, and I'm not saying it.

"Come on! It rhymes with . . ." He thinks for a minute. "Huh. It doesn't rhyme with anything."

"I'm not saying I'm sorry!" I say. "It's not my fault. Wrangler Brett even said so."

"Yeah, but if you think Kansas won't pass you, then it is your problem. If you're not going to fix things with her by apologizing, I suppose you have another idea?"

"No," I say. "Wrangler Brett says Kansas needs to lighten up." Goose trots up and we stop to pet him. I look around for Kansas but don't see her. "She doesn't even laugh at Goose. I mean, she gets tired of him hanging around and *he* doesn't even talk, so there's probably no hope she'll ever like me."

Dad calls me on the walkie-talkie again. "I'm coming!" I say, feeling a little annoyed at him.

"If you learned to butt her, that might make her laugh," JT says.

I make a face and straighten Goose's bandanna.

"Or . . ." says JT with a funny smile. "Maybe she'd laugh if Goose started talking."

"Right," I say.

But then JT starts chewing on his thumbnail. I know what that means: he's thinking hard about something.

"Why not?" he says, almost like he's saying it to himself. "It's not like I have anything better to do."

"What? What are you going to do?"

"Tomorrow," he says, "the Gooser will talk. Oh yes. He will talk."

After that, even though I beg him to tell me more, the only thing JT will say is, "All will be made clear tomorrow."

6. Goose, Goose . . . Duck!

The next day it rains. And rains. And rains. Nobody is happy about it. My mom is not happy because the party is tomorrow, and if the rain doesn't clear up, "it will be a complete and utter disaster." She keeps saying that every two minutes, and every time she gets to the word *disaster*, she puts her head in her hands. My dad is not happy because my mom is frizzled out. Liza is not happy because, well, she's Liza and she's a pain, so it's like any other day with her.

But the rain is worst of all for me, because it means the riding test has to be canceled. It's Tuesday. We're exactly halfway through our stay, and I'm still not on the dusty trail. Or the muddy trail. Or any trail, with any horses! How am I supposed to win the Rider Show-Off if I never get any real cowgirl practice? I slump and moan about that until my dad asks me to pick up the room I'm sharing with Liza.

"The cleaning crew is coming soon, and there is so much junk on the floor right now that they won't be able to get to the beds to change the sheets," he says, following me to our room.

I get down on my hands and knees and use my arms like a bulldozer to make a pathway to the bed. "Done!" I say.

"I don't think so," he says.

"I like it this way! It's just like my room back home."

"I don't. I almost slipped on one of your books when I tried to get to Liza's crib."

"Okay, then I'll bulldoze a path to the crib."

"No," he says, all serious. "You will pick up your clothes and books and hairbrush and towel and tiny plastic horses with their tiny plastic riders and put them away so you don't endanger me, your sister, or the nice people from Lazy K."

I go into the room and close the door.

"And do a good job of it!" he says.

I don't know why's he's so crabby, but I open a dresser drawer and then use my arms like a front loader to scoop up everything that's on my floor and dump it into the open drawer. But that only takes about a minute, and if I go back out into the living room now, it will make my dad naturally curious about how I could clean up so fast. I flump down on the bed to read.

After a few minutes, JT opens the door. "You done?" he says. I sweep my arm through the air so he can see how done the room is. "Good. Let's motor."

Sometimes I think that JT speaks his own language. "Huh?" I say.

"I'm springing you, getting you out of here, away from the evil man who looks like our dad."

"There's a happiness," I say. "What's wrong with him, anyway?"

"Cabin fever," he says.

JT sprints through the rain to the barn and I follow him as fast as I can. Which makes me all out of breath. "What . . . are . . . we . . . going . . . to . . . do?" I pant, following JT behind a stack of hay.

JT still has all his breath. "We're going to try to get Kansas to lighten up."

"How?"

"You'll see. You just get Goose and meet me back here. Catch!" He tosses me a bag of bread crusts. "Use these. I saw another wrangler feeding some to Goose earlier. He loves bread."

Because it's raining, there aren't any trail rides and all the horses are still in their stalls. I clomp down the aisle between them and ask Wrangler Dena if she's seen Goose. "Most likely he's with Kansas," she says.

"Where's Kansas?"

"Couldn't tell you that."

I finally find her and Goose in the tack room, which is full of saddles and bridles and smells like my cowboy boots but even stronger and better than that. Kansas is trying to clean a saddle, but Goose keeps bumping her arm. She looks up at me and frowns.

"I'm not going to stay," I blurt. "I just came for Goose. I thought him and me could play a little."

"Good luck getting him away from me."

I hold out the crusts. Right away Goose trots over. I give him a little bit and then take a step back into the hallway. Goose follows me, without looking back. I give him another. He follows me all the way back to JT, butting me whenever he thinks I'm not giving him the crusts fast enough.

JT grins when he sees Goose. "All right." He pulls some twine and Dad's walkie-talkie out of his pocket.

"How did you get that?"

"I just told Dad that you and I wanted to use them and promised him I'd be responsible for you. You still have yours, right?" I nod. JT gets down on his knees and tries to tie dad's walkie-talkie around Goose's neck.

Goose is pretty strong for a baby goat. I wrap my arms around him and hold him as best I can, but he wriggles his head all over the place, trying to get to my bread-crust bag.

"Hold him still!" JT says.

"I'm trying!" I say.

"Give him another treat."

"Okay, but tie the walkie-talkie on quick. He gulps his food!"

"You just do your part and don't worry about me," JT says.

After a little more wrestling around with Goose, JT gets the walkie-talkie on him, then rearranges the bandanna so that it hides the walkie-talkie.

"When are you going to tell me what you're doing?" I ask.

"I told you. Goose here is going to make Kansas lighten up."

"How? He's around her all the time and she doesn't smile."

JT grins and points to my walkie-talkie. "Easy. He's going to tell her a joke."

Now I get it! JT is going to talk into my walkie-talkie and his voice will come out the walkie-talkie that's hidden under Goose's bandanna so it will *seem* like Goose is talking. Sometimes JT's brain is a miracle.

"I want to help," I say.

"When we let Goose go, he'll go find Kansas. You follow him and try to find someplace to hide where you can see Kansas and Goose. I'll follow at a distance and stay out of sight, but I'll still be able to see you. Give me the thumbs-up when Goose finds Kansas. Then I'll make Goose talk."

"Should we let Goose go now?"

JT nods. "We want to do this while Kansas is still here. Otherwise it will be too hard to stay out of sight."

I let go of Goose, and he right away nibbles at my pocket where I have the treats. I push him away. "Go on, Goose. Go find Kansas." But he won't go.

"Give him the rest of the treats," JT says. "Then show him your pocket is empty."

After I do that, Goose finally leaves. Glad that he didn't know about the sugar cubes I have in my shirt pocket for

Terco, I follow Goose back down the long barn hallway around the corner and see him go into the tack room.

I'm almost to the door when I hear Kansas say, "Move, Goose. I'm done in here." I stick my thumb up, hoping that JT is watching, and jump into the closest stall to hide.

Just then Kansas comes out of the tack room. Goose, who is right behind her, bleats out, "He-e-ey, Kansas. I got a go-o-od one for you-ou." Only really it's just JT who is faking a goat voice. Except he's doing it all wrong because he's talking like a girl goat would talk instead of like a boy goat would talk.

Kansas stops so fast that Goose butts into her without even meaning to. She turns around and squinches up her eyes at Goose, who is sniffing at Kansas's boots. Goose says, "Why did the squirrel fall out of the tre-e-e?" Before Goose is even done asking that question, Kansas has found the walkie-talkie and used her pocketknife to cut it off Goose's neck.

"Mary Margaret, I know it's you," she yells, looking down the hall in the wrong direction. That gives me the chance to duck down so she won't be able to see me.

I don't say anything. I don't even breathe. So far, Kansas has not smiled and I don't think she's going to. Which means this is not going exactly the way JT planned.

"Are you coming out or do I have to come find you?"

I think about this. Kansas sounds pretty mad. Some people hit when they are mad. If I go out, there's still a way to run if she turns out to be a hitter. But if she finds me here in the stall, I'll be trapped. I wish there was a secret door that I could use to escape, but I don't see one. I stand up and take baby steps out of the stall.

Kansas is waiting for me. There's a bridle over her shoulder and her hands are on her hips. "You think you're pretty smart, don't you?"

"Well, no," I say, because it's really JT who is so smart this time.

But Kansas isn't even listening. "So smart that you could fool me into thinking that Goose here can talk. What do you take me for?"

"Nothing," I say. "It was a joke."

"Oh, so it was like 'let's see how easy it is to make a fool out of a dumb country girl'? Ha ha, oh, that's a good one! *Very* funny," she says. I know from the way she says it that she doesn't think it was funny at all. She slaps the walkie-talkie into my hand and says, "No matter what you do to me, I have to be decent to you because you're a guest. But do me a favor. Other than for riding lessons in the corral, keep yourself and those ridiculous red boots away from me. Compren-day?"

Compren-day is kind of like "know what I mean" in Spanish. I nod.

She spins around and stomps away.

From down the hall in the other direction JT bleats, "He-e-y, the boots aren't that b-a-a-ad."

"This is all your fault," I say as he walks toward me. "It was your idea and then it went backward."

JT looks in the direction that Kansas disappeared and shrugs. "Yeah, it really did. My mistake was in thinking she had a sense of humor. She doesn't. Oh, well."

"This has made things between me and Kansas worse than ever! Before she at least let me hang around, so I had the chance for her to like me. Now she hates me—and my boots!"

"Why do you even care? In a few days we'll leave here and you'll never see her again. You don't usually care what everyone else thinks about you or what you wear. Why now?"

"Because she has to be my friend! She just has to!"

"But why?"

"Because I decided it. I decided when I met her that we would be friends—and I'm no *quitter*!"

As he walks away he shakes his head and says, "I don't get it."

I don't really get it, either. I've finally met someone I admire more than I admire myself. But the more Kansas gets to know me, the *less* she seems to like me. And if she doesn't like me, then maybe I'm wrong about all the things I admire about myself. I have always thought there are a lot of things to like about me. But maybe there are only a few. I put the lid on my brain right then before the next thought can drop into it. Because the next thought might be, Maybe there aren't any things at all.

7. Unfamiliar Territory

All I want right then is to find a secret spot to be by myself. That's hard to do because it's raining and all the wranglers are looking for chores to do inside, where it's warm and dry.

I finally find an empty box stall with clean straw. The sliding door that leads to the pasture is open. I sit in the corner of the stall and watch the rain come down and down, which is how I feel—down and down. After a while, Smokey, a gray barn cat, wanders in and curls up in my lap.

Pretty soon it starts to feel cozy, with the sounds of Smokey purring and the rain pattering down on the roof above me. I take a few deep breaths and breathe in the barn. The funny thing about barn smell is that it's really lots of smells smushed together. Closing my eyes and breathing even deeper, I try to pull the smells apart. There's straw, fresh sawdust, leather, grain, hay, damp wood, horse, cat, wet dirt . . . Smokey purrs. The rain comes down. And without even meaning to, I fall asleep.

I don't know how long I sleep before something

prickles at my cheek. When I open my eyes, I am staring into two big black nostrils. "Eeep!" I peep, trying to push myself away by scrabbling my feet. But my back is already against the wall. I'm trapped.

The horse takes a step back and I can see more than just its black nose. I can see enough of the horse to know that it's Twister who's standing between me and the door to safety. He's soaking wet—and even bigger than I remember.

He arches his neck toward me again and snorts a loud, wet snort. It means:

> *Fee, Fi, Fo, Fit,*
> *I smell Mary Margaret!*
> *What's she doing*
> *In my stall?*
> *She belongs*
> *In the hall!*

My heart is taking running jumps, like it's trying to find a way out of my body. My scared brain is running laps around my skull. I try to remember everything I've learned about how to act around horses. *Move slow. Talk quiet.* Or was it *don't talk at all*? They know when you're afraid, so *don't be afraid.*

Too bad Lefty never said how to *not* be afraid when you already are.

Just then Smokey opens his eyes to see what's going on, then closes them again. That calms me down because cats are smart, and if Smokey isn't afraid, maybe that means Twister isn't making a plan for trampling me.

"Nice Twister. Nice boy." My voice comes out quiet but shaky. "I'm sorry I came into your stall without asking permission. My brother JT hates it when I do that. But I didn't know it was your box stall. You were in a different one yesterday, so it's not my fault I'm in the wrong place. What are you trying to do, trick me?" He snorts again. I wonder how much of what I'm saying he understands. Horses are one of the planet's most intelligent animals (I read that in a book), so he probably understands some of it. At least I hope he does.

"I gave you a treat, remember? I sure hope you don't mind me talking. It's just what I do when I get nervous. Oh, wait. I probably shouldn't have told you that! Now you know I'm scared. Forget that part. Actually, I talk pretty much all the time. Now, if you'll just move over a step, I'll be leaving."

To get to the door, I have to get past Twister. So I take a little scoot toward the door. He watches me but doesn't move over at all. Instead, he lays back his ears, throws his head, and stamps his foot. I'm not sure what that means, but it looks like a horsey temper tantrum to me. I freeze. He shakes his glossy mane then lowers his head and sniffs my shoulder, then my neck. I freeze harder so I can sit stiller. When he gets to my shirt pocket, he nibbles at it with his lips. Suddenly I understand horse language. Twister wants Terco's sugar cubes! I reach for my pocket but then stop. What if he still won't let me by even after I give him the cubes? I need to be smarter than him.

Slowly I take one of the cubes out of my pocket. The door I'm trying to get to is on my left side, so I hold the cube in my right hand and put out my right arm beside my body as far as it will go. To get to the cube, Twister has to step away from the door. The cube is small, so he eats it quickly, but I have two more cubes. I do the same thing two more times. Each time while he's busy reaching for the cube and swallowing it, I'm busy scootering my behind toward the door. I keep Smokey in my lap the whole time because I don't want to leave him behind, even if he isn't afraid. It's a slow way to get to the door, but my plan works. I finally make it onto the cement in the barn hallway. I even remember to close the stall door behind me.

The cement isn't as comfortable as the soft straw, but at least it's safe. I lie on it for a few minutes until I don't feel so unwound and wobbly. From far away, I hear *ahh-choo!* And then *crik-crik-crik-squeak, crik-crik-crik-squeak.* Which means that it's my dad, pushing Liza's squeaky stroller. *Ahh-CHOO!*

I don't want my dad to know where I've been, so I hop up and dust off my pants.

In another minute, they come around the corner. "Hi, Dad," I say, trying to make my voice normal. "What are you doing here?"

"Looking for—*AHHHH-CHOO!*—you," he says, wiping at his eyes.

"I thought you weren't supposed to come into the barn."

He sneezes again then holds up his Kleenex. "I'm not." Then he has a big sneezing fit and he can't even stop long enough to say another word. He just points at me and then at the door and he gets out of there quick like a bunny—a sneezy bunny.

We start walking back to the cabin. When he finally stops sneezing, he tells me that he came looking for me because he couldn't get me on the walkie-talkie. "I thought either you were lying unconscious in some ditch, or that your unit needed new batteries," he says, sniffling. "I'm glad to see it's the latter."

He hands the batteries to me. "I don't want them," I say, giving them back.

"The walkie-talkie won't work without them. You need them." He takes the walkie-talkie and pops off the back so he can change the batteries.

"I don't care if it doesn't work. I *want* it not to work! That dumb thing just gets in my way and spooks the animals. Besides, I don't even need it! Nothing is going to happen to me here, Dad. I'm not going to trip off a cliff or fry in a wildfire or drown in the rain! It's not the Wild West. It's just the dinky Lazy K Ranch. There aren't even any cattle rustlers."

"Wild boars, aliens, a plague of locusts, could descend upon the land," he says, waving his arms through the air. I know he's trying to be funny but I'm not in the mood.

When he sees I'm not, he gets serious. "Look, I don't feel comfortable letting you roam the range, even a dinky range, without it."

"But we've been here for days and nothing has happened!"

"That doesn't mean nothing will. What then?"

I think about what just happened with Twister and how I got myself out. "Then maybe I'll just figure it out myself," I say, raising my chin. "I can do that, you know. I'm not a baby anymore."

He squats down in front of me, which I like, because it means I'm looking down at him instead of him looking down at me. "Mary Margaret, there are many things I'm sure you can figure out," he says. "But you are only nine and this is unfamiliar territory."

I feel stuck right then. I can prove to him that I can handle things—if I tell him about what just happened in the stall with Twister. But if I tell him, it might make him even more nervous about me roaming the ranch.

Telling him is too risky, so I decide not to. But then, besides feeling stuck, I also feel mad. Stuck + mad = frustrated, so I guess that's what I am right now. I cross my arms over my chest and stamp my foot. "I'd rather go home than keep wearing that stupid thing."

He raises his eyebrows. "You'd rather go home?"

I nod once, fast. I hope he still has too much allergy water in his eyes to notice that I have tears in mine.

He puts his arms on my shoulders and says, "There's something wrong with this picture. You wouldn't give up being here just because of the walkie-talkies."

Everything is wrong with the picture! But all I say is, "It's not fair!"

"What's not fair?"

"It's not fair that I haven't gotten to go on a trail ride. I'm good enough, it's just that Terco won't listen to me!" I poke my finger at my walkie-talkie. "It's not fair that I have to use those stupid walkie-talkies."

"You've already said."

"And it's not fair that . . . it's not fair that . . . Nobody likes me!" I'm doing nonstop blinking to keep the tears from spilling out of my eyes.

My dad tilts his head at me. "Nobody likes you? Nobody at all?"

"Well, not Kansas. I've been nice to her. I've given her lots of chances to get to know me. I've been myself, like Mom told me to. I kept her company while she did chores, but she says I talk too much!"

My dad honks into a Kleenex. "It's hard, especially when you so badly want that person to like you."

Right then my blinking stops working, and the tears dribble out of my eyes and slide over my cheeks. My dad puts his arms around me and I lean against him. "Nobody's ever not liked me before," I sob-say. "And that's what's not fair because I haven't even done anything wrong." I leave out the part about me maybe hurting Kansas's feelings. After all, she hurt mine, so we're even on that. "Plus there's a lot about me to like, I think." I pull away a little so I can look into his eyes. "Isn't there, Dad? A lot to like about me?"

He smiles and—*yuck!*—tries to use the Kleenex he just honked into to mop up my tears! "Dad!" I say.

He looks at the Kleenex and then at me. "Oh, sorry," he says. He shoves the Kleenex into his pocket. "There is a lot to like about you. There most definitely is. But not everyone you meet is going to want to be your friend. Kansas is older than you."

"I know. Plus she says farm kids grow up faster. She thinks I'm mollycoddled."

"Which is why you don't want the walkie-talkie."

I shrug. "It makes her think I'm a kid."

"And if she didn't think of you as little, maybe she'd like you."

"Uh-huh."

"We love you the way you are," he says. "But if all your talking bothers Kansas and you want to be friends, then you could dial back the talking a little—just do it less and let her talk more."

"But she doesn't talk more!"

"Then she probably likes it quiet. But even compromising on the talking might not make Kansas like you. You can't force Kansas to like you any more than we can force you to like your baby sister."

"Oh," I say. My shoulders sag a little when I hear this disappointing news.

I know my dad can tell how I'm feeling because he says, "But you *can* prove you're bigger than Kansas seems to think you are."

Uh-oh. I know what's coming next. The way I ended up with Hershey was that I started helping out around the house without even being asked, which wasn't that easy because I didn't have any experience with that. Anyway, helping out showed my mom and dad I was getting older on the inside, and not just older and bigger on the outside. Because it's possible to get *older* without *growing up*, which I never knew before.

I'm right about what's coming next. My dad says, "Watch what she does around the ranch, because those are the things that will impress her and earn her respect. Don't stop being who you are. Just show her you can *do* as much as you can talk."

"And then she'll like me."

"Possibly," he says. "Respect can lead to friendship, eventually. No guarantees, though."

Walking back to the cabin, I make sure no one is around and then I reach for my dad's hand. He smiles and switches to pushing Liza's stroller with one hand so he has a free hand for me. When I was little, I had to hold his hand because I wasn't that good at walking. But now I do it because I want to. And even though I'm nine and close to completely grown up, my hand still feels a tiny bit small in his.

8. Poop-Out at the Old Corral

Weenie-weenie Wednesday,
The middle of our stay.
One thing I know for sure
Today I'll ride away!

I spear a hunk of pancake and fork it into my mouth, feeling as bright as the sun that popped up this morning. Right away everyone catches my powerful good mood. My mom is happy because it's not going to rain on party day. My dad is happy because he is going to the party, too, which means he has a night off from watching Liza. JT is out on a run, and he's always happy when he runs.

Liza does not catch my good mood, but she doesn't count because she's never happy.

On the way out to the barn after breakfast, I think about what my dad said that maybe Kansas would want to be friends with me, after I impress her. I make up a plan on how to do that. Then I make up another poem. Because that's just the way I am.

Maybe. Possibly.
Probably. It could be.
Oh, so hope-filly!
Best friends—her and me!

It's twice as good as a normal poem because besides rhyming, it has a pun.

I see JT at the hitching post, drinking water from a hose. Lefty is coming from the other direction, leading Bob the horse. But once Bob sees the hose, he puts on the brakes.

"Hi!" I say to Lefty. "What are you doing?"

He jerks his head toward the hose. "Bob and me and the hose are going to spend some quality time together," he says. "Just as soon as your brother's done."

JT wipes his mouth with the back of his hand and shuts off the hose. "Done," he says.

"I thought Bob was afraid of the hose," I say.

Lefty ties Bob's lead rope to the hitching post. "Less afraid today than he was yesterday. We've been working on it, making good progress."

"You want me to turn on the hose again?" JT asks.

Lefty shakes his head. "It'll be a while before we try that." He picks up the hose and Bob sidesteps away from it. "Easy, Bob," Lefty says. With his free hand, he rubs Bob's neck, then slowly rubs the hose over Bob's chest. Bob lifts his head like he's getting ready to back away and the whites of his eyes show for a second, but then Bob lets Lefty do it.

"Good man, Bob," Lefty says, putting the hose down and giving Bob a piece of apple.

"That's it?" I ask. "That's the progress?"

"Sure is," Lefty says. "When we first started, Bob wouldn't even walk up to the hose. After I got him doing that, I starting rubbing the hose on the bottom of his legs. Now we're all the way up to his chest." Bob bumps his face against Lefty's chest and Lefty gives him another hunk of apple. "Lizard steps, eh, Bob? Don't need those giant leaps. All you need is to inch along."

Like me and Kansas, I think. Only I must have thought those words out loud without even knowing I did, because Lefty says, "That's the only way to get anywhere with her—nice and slow."

"Why's she so prickly, anyway?" I ask. JT gives me a look that means, *It's none of your business.* I give him a look right back that means, *What's your problem?*

Lefty looks at the ground and rubs the back of his neck. "Well now, I know more about critters than I do about girls," he says. "You take Bob, here. He lets you know what he's afraid of. But some critters are just the opposite. They hide their fears and plunge ahead. Just the way they are. But once you know that about them, you can work with it."

"If they hide them, how do you ever figure out what they are afraid of?" asks JT.

Lefty shrugs. "It doesn't matter much what it is. What matters is that you know they're scared, so you're a little more careful with them. Maybe you move real slow and coax 'em a little."

I heave a big sigh. "Yeah, but I asked about *Kansas*."

"I told you," Lefty says, grinning. "I don't know much about girls." He glances over at JT. "Do you?"

"Not really."

"Yes, you do!" I say. "He has two sisters and a mom!" I explain to Lefty. "And we have a girl pet rabbit. He even talks to girls on the phone."

JT shoots me a dirty look, but then he says, "Yeah, none of that makes any difference. I still don't understand girls."

I roll my eyes and tap my finger on the side of my head. "He's a little *S-L-O-W* after he goes running. It takes a while for his brain to stop jiggling," I say to Lefty. I wait for JT to zing me back. But he just chews on his thumbnail and looks toward the barn, where Kansas is—and where I'm headed.

When I get there, Kansas is cleaning out stalls.

"Good morning!" I say, sitting down on my favorite stack of hay.

Kansas grunts.

I press my heels into the hay and clack the tips of my boots together. "I have my boots on and I am ready to help!"

Kansas leans on her pitchfork and looks at me, then at my boots. "Is that right?"

"That's right. Because, as my grandpa always says, 'The only good company is working company.'"

"Those stalls need to be mucked out," she says.

"You mean . . . you want me to . . . fork up the dung?"

Kansas just looks at me. Which I guess means yes.

I look down at my shiny red boots. I've gotten very attached to them. Even though I've only had them for a few days, we've been through a lot together. Like riding a horse for the first time. "Well," I say slowly, "I was thinking more about something like feeding or sweeping." Something I can do without getting my boots dirty, I think.

"Feeding's done," she says. "So's the sweeping."

Kansas swings her gold-rope hair over her shoulder and waits for me to answer. I think about how she rides spunky horses and doesn't have to carry a walkie-talkie or even be home in time for dinner. Holding up a pitchfork with one hand, she looks a little like the Statue of Liberty, with six earrings sparkling in the light. I want her to like me. And I guess I want her respect, but it's just that . . . well, these are my beautiful boots!

She puts the pitchfork back on the wall. "That's what I thought," she says. "Just another city kid. You say you love horses, but you don't really. Not when it comes to the work. You like the idea of it, is all. You'd rather be shopping."

I leap off the hay like it's a slide on a hot July day and I'm wearing shorts. "I do too love horses," I say, reaching for the pitchfork. "And I *hate* shopping. Ask anybody. They'll tell you."

The pitchfork is heavier on the fork end than on the

handle end. When I lift it off its peg on the wall, the fork end drops to the floor right in front of Kansas. *Clang-g-g!* But then I heave it up again and figure out how to carry it. I'll show her! I'll show Kansas that I'm not just another city kid. I'll prove that I'm not just another *any* kind of kid. I am myself, and there is a lot about me to like. "Where do I start?" I ask.

She points to two stalls. "There. Use that wheelbarrow over by the door. Pick up the manure and then just put the wheelbarrow back. Someone else will dump it. Riding tests start in a little while. I'll meet you at the corral." She doesn't seem impressed yet, but she will be. She'll *have* to be once she sees how good I am at this.

Only it doesn't work out quite that way.

I wait until she leaves before tucking my tassels into my boots. (I'm *not* a city kid. I just like my boots, same as any wrangler.) Then I march into the first stall. Horse dung comes out in little balls, which I did not know before coming to the Lazy K. There are just two piles in the stall, so it shouldn't be too much work. But it does stink in there. So I try holding my breath. But the balls keep falling through the fork part of the pitchfork. It takes so long to get just one ball from one pile onto the pitchfork that after about a minute of trying, I stumble out of the stall, sucking for breath.

The stall still needs to get mucked out somehow, if I want to impress Kansas, which I do. Next I try holding my nose with one hand and holding the pitchfork with the

89

other and stabbing at the balls with the poky end of the pitchfork. That doesn't work because the balls break apart as soon as I try to lift them.

Wrangler Brett walks by and sees me trying. "Scoop the whole pile at once, and just a little of the straw underneath it, too. It helps everything hang together, if you know what I'm saying."

"Thanks," I say.

I hold my nose with my left hand and try to scoop with the other, but my one arm isn't strong enough to pick up the whole pile at once. Finally, I give up on holding my nose and just squinch it instead, the way I sometimes squinch my eyes. Now I can breathe but not so deep that I smell the stink. I use both hands on the pitchfork and I try the way Wrangler Brett says. It works! I am mucking out stalls, just like a real wrangler!

Because I am a fast learner, I muck out the next stall zippety fast. I stand back, lean on my pitchfork, and sigh a little sigh of happiness. I wish Kansas could see the job I have done.

That's when I remember she said she'd meet me in the corral for riding tests, and I need to get over there. Today is the day I'm going to pass and get out on the dusty trail! But when I'm putting the wheelbarrow back like she told me, it hits a big crack in the barn floor and tips to the side. I stop the tipping before the wheelbarrow goes all the way over, but I pull too hard and the wheelbarrow tips to the other side. This time it's tipping faster than I can stop it, so it crashes all the way to the floor and there's nothing I can do but say, "No, no, no!" as all my hard work tumbles out onto the barn floor.

That's when I discover why cowboy boots have pointy toes. It's so that you can kick a dumb wheelbarrow when it ruins all your hard work. "Cussing, cussing, double cussing such-and-such!" I say as I kick it again and again. "Now I'm never going to get over to the corral."

Just then Lefty walks by. "Need some help there?"

"I mucked out two stalls all by myself," I say. "And I did a good job of it, too, and then this went and happened and now I'm going to be too late to take the riding test and I'm going to be stuck in that cussing-cussing kiddie corral." All those words talk my tears up to the edges of my eyes but I don't want to let them out because I'm pretty sure that Kansas never cries, so I don't want to either.

Lefty sets up the wheelbarrow and says, "Look, this won't take me but half a minute to clean up, being the old pro that I am. You did your part—a lot more than most guests do—so now get on over to the corral."

I stand there wondering if I should ask him if he's sure. If I ask him, it'll give him a chance to change his mind and I don't want him to change his mind.

Lefty reads my thinking and says, "Yes, I'm sure. Now git. And if you know anything about cowboys at all, you know that when one of 'em tells you to git, you *git*."

I'm running out of the barn almost before he's done talking. "Thanks, Lefty!" I yell.

I'm all out of breath when I get to the corral fence, but I don't even wait to get it back before I yell to Kansas, "I cleaned—I mean *mucked out*—those stalls like you wanted me to."

Kansas waves once from where she's standing in the middle of the corral, like she's flicking a fly away, and then bends over to pin a ribbon on a boy. When he walks out of the corral, he has a big smile on his face, probably only because he doesn't know what the yellow ribbon means. Since I've been hanging around the barn asking questions, I know the ribbons are a code for how good you ride. Anyone who has a ribbon can go on a trail ride, but a yellow ribbon means you aren't allowed to go any faster on your horse than a walk. Green means you can walk and trot. Purple means you can walk, trot, and canter. So that kid can get all excited about having a yellow ribbon if he wants, but I know better.

"Kansas, did you hear what I said, about the stalls? I did it!"

She leads Terco over to me. "Yeah, I heard you."

"It wasn't even hard, once I got the hang of it. I did them both. All two of them." And then I tell her about all the different ways I tried and how none of them worked that well. I leave out the part about the wheelbarrow tipping over.

"Uh-huh," she says, holding Terco so I can get on. But I can tell she's not really listening because it's the same "uh-huh" that my dad uses when he's reading a book.

Sometimes, if the book is really good, I can even get an extra cookie by asking him for it while he's reading.

Kansas lets go of Terco and gives her a slap on the rump. "Take her out to the rail and have her walk around a few times."

Today I feel like Terco will finally understand that I have to—have to!—get out on that trail, where the wind can blow back my hair and Terco and I can gallop as one, free on the range, just the way it is in the movies. I'm sure she will obey me and I will pass the test this time.

While we're walking I tell her everything I told Kansas about mucking out the stalls. Then I tell her all about the big party that my mom is helping with and how the decorations are all going to be blue and yellow, even though I think the party should have an Appaloosa theme, with brown and black and white decorations, because those are the colors Terco is and they look good on her, but my mom won't change her mind. And I tell her how happy my mom is that the weather is nice, and how she said she could cross out *bad weather* on her list of things she's obsessed with, because it's party day and it's not going to rain.

Before we get to the gate, I start kicking Terco really hard so she'll know I mean business. Terco looks longingly at the gate, but she keeps walking. Which means I am doing good!

And then I tell Terco how I had a egg burry toe for breakfast and how I had never had one before but that it tasted pretty much like scrambled eggs except they were wrapped in a thin pancake thingy and that made them look long and skinny and a little like a toe, I guess, and that must be why they are called burry toes.

"It's a *burrito*," yells Kansas from the middle of the corral. "Not a burry toe."

"Oh," I say. And then I say to Terco, "I think burry toe is more interesting, don't you?"

"Cut to D and then back to B," she yells, pointing to the letters painted along the inside of the corral, all spaced out. This is good news for me! It means that I've passed the first part of the test, which is to keep Terco going. Now I get to try to pass the next part—making Terco go where I want her to go. Or actually, where Kansas tells me to.

On the way to D, I tell Terco all about JT and how bored he is and then about Liza and how sometimes I feel like she ruins our family and how I thought for a whole afternoon that my mom was pregnant again, but she really isn't. We're almost to D, so I lay the reins on Terco's neck but she won't turn. She just stays close to the fence and keeps walking.

"Turn her," Kansas yells.

"I'm trying!" I lay the reins against her neck harder, but she ignores me.

"Try tugging on the inside rein, too," she says.

I try and try, but Terco has another idea. Her idea is that she has a habit of walking in a big circle, around and around the corral, and that's what she's going to do. I try to talk her out of it. I try to talk sweet to her. My words don't change her mind. Neither do my arms. Terco's mind and her neck are stronger than my arms are.

"It's no wonder she won't do what you ask. All your talking confuses her," Kansas says.

I clap my hand over my mouth because right then I remember that I was going to *try* to talk a little less.

"Help me," I say, through my hand.

"What?"

I move my hand. "Then help me!"

"You have to be able to do this on your own before you go on a trail ride," Kansas says, walking up to Terco. "Maybe tomor—"

I know what she's going to say next and I have to stop her from saying it before it's too late. "It's not me! It's Terco! She won't cooperate. Maybe there's something really wrong with her."

Kansas scowls up at me. "Terco's a good little horse. Ask any of the hundred riders who've ridden her this year."

"Well, maybe she's just gone sour, like a carton of old milk."

"I don't think so," Kansas says.

"Just—just—" But before I can get out what I want to say, my breathing goes all funny. It's like my body knows how upset my heart is and it's trying to be gentle to it. "Please don't tell me I can't ride. I have to go out—just once. I have to!" I beg. "Horses are in my blood—even in my bones." And then I say the truest thing of all. "They are in my *very soul.*"

Kansas puts her hand on my leg and says, "You're right that it's not your fault. Your arms just aren't strong enough yet. They're still too twiggy. Next year, when—"

"They are too strong!" I say, curling them up and making a muscle. "Just not right now. They are tired from cleaning out the stalls. I know I could get her to do what I wanted if my arms weren't all rubbery from being tired!"

"Sorry, Princess," she says.

When my heart is jittering around in my chest it's like it jitters all my thoughts around, too, and everything gets mixed together in me—Terco being her stupid, stubborn self, and my not being able to ride, and Kansas not liking me. "You know how much I want to ride! You're just being mean because you don't like me. You never liked me!" I lean onto Terco's neck and swing my leg over her rump so I can slide out of the saddle. I hand Kansas the reins. "Just forget about it. I don't care. All this dude-ranch stuff is dumb anyway. It's like a bunch of old people playing dress-up. It's not *real*."

Every word I say feels like a rock I'm throwing at her. And it feels good. Right then, it's true that I don't care. I might have cared at first, but now I don't. It's like when you play outside in winter and your nose hurts when it first gets cold. But then pretty soon you can't feel the hurt because your nose is so cold, it's numb.

I stomp across the corral, not even caring what I step in. I've been friendly. I've tried to do what Kansas told me to with Terco. And I mucked out two stalls, all by myself to impress her and make her like me. I stop and turn around because there is something my jittery, quivery heart wants to say to her. It wants me to say, *Why? Why don't you like me?* But when I open my mouth, all that comes out is, "I picked up poop for you." Which sounds really dumb, even to me.

He's not coming," my mom says, when I walk in the door. She snaps closed her cell phone and starts tossing it up in the air and catching it. Party Central has moved from my parents' bedroom to the kitchen. The table is covered with my mom's notes and phone numbers and schedules. All week she's been scribbling on sticky notes, things like *Brown—no nuts!* and *Vegetarian?* and *Table skirt*. The notes are in long rows and organized by color. Notes about food are all on yellow stickees and notes about the entertainment are on blue ones. There's also a giant schedule that tells how the party is going to go: *Appetizers, Entertainment, Dinner, Celebration Ceremony, Dancing.*

"Mom," I say.

My mom looks at me, but I can tell that she doesn't really see me. "My magician is doing a disappearing act," she says, like she can't believe it. She walks over to the table and pulls off the blue sticky notes and crumples them all up. "Which means the guests are going to be sitting around staring at each other, thinking it would be more fun to watch *grass grow* than to be at this party! And my client is *not* going to be happy. Not happy at all."

"Lil," says my dad. "Breathe."

My mom starts pacing around the table. "Oh! I'm breathing, all right!"

"Mom," I say again. I take a step toward her.

My dad swings his arm out in front of my chest, like a crossing guard, to stop me. "I just want to talk to her," I say.

He bends over and whispers, "Look at her. She's breathing, which is good. But she's breathing fire—not so good. Can you ask me instead?"

I shrug. "Okay." He follows me to my room, where I plop down on the bed. I'm ready to spill it all out on him, everything that happened. I say, "Well, Kansas—"

My dad puts his finger over his lips and points to the crib, where there's a lump called Liza sleeping. I get what he's saying, which is "don't bother the baby." First I shouldn't bother Mom and now I shouldn't bother the baby. And then this very big question rolls through my brain in capital letters, like this: WHAT ABOUT ME? But I don't actually ask that question, because I know my dad will try to prove they do think about me, when I know that they don't. Much. Suddenly I don't even want to tell him about everything that just happened with Kansas.

"What was it you wanted to talk about?" he whispers.

"Nothing," I whisper back.

My dad looks worried. "Are you feeling all right?"

"I just don't feel like talking."

He raises his eyebrows at me. "I don't know whether to call the doctor or the *Chicago Tribune*. You—the queen of talk—not feeling like talking? That's breaking news!"

"I just want to be left alone right now." I'm getting tired of whispering, which seems like more work than talking, even though talking is louder.

JT pokes his head in the door. "Are you guys about done?" he whispers. "Mom says she needs our brains."

Dad nods toward the door. "She just needs your brain," he says. "Not your problems. So can you wait for a few more minutes to be alone?"

I roll my eyes. Since I'm not really alone in that room anyway, because of Liza, I follow him and JT back to the living room.

Mom doesn't even wait for us to sit down before she says, "All right, everyone. I need entertainment for tonight. Let's hear your ideas."

My dad tugs on his cap. "What about the wranglers? Maybe they could sing."

"They're waiting tables tonight. Next?"

"I could probably throw together some kind of movie," says JT, "but without my computer and my other stuff, I can't do any of that. Sorry, Mom."

My mom taps her pad of paper with her pencil tip. "Keep thinking. Mary Margaret, what've you got?"

I look down and mutter, "Dirty red boots, a dumb walkie-talkie, and a squashed dream."

Nobody even pays attention to the squashed-dream part. Instead, right away JT says, "Hey, maybe I can figure out something with the walkie-talkies again. Maybe like making Goose sing."

"It has to be a crowd-pleaser," my mom says. "I want them to mingle, so it has to be something that will make people want to talk about it afterward. Like when I was in fourth grade, we had an assembly where a hypnotist hypnotized kids and made them squat, cluck, and waddle like ducks. Maybe something like that."

My dad snaps his fingers. "Fortune-telling!"

"Yes!" says my mom. "Perfect!"

I just sit and watch while Mom and Dad and JT figure everything out. They finally decide on "The Bearded Wonder" as the name of the "fortune-teller"—Goose. The plan is that Goose will follow Kansas as she walks around the party. Goose will tell guests what will happen to them in the future, but really it will be Lefty doing the talking from some hiding place. Normally I would be right in the middle of all the talking, because I am a great idea maker. But this time I'm not because my mind keeps bumping around and bouncing off my own problems.

At the end of the family meeting, Mom gives everyone a job. She asks me to ask Kansas to help with the fortune-telling. I am still not in a talking mood and I don't feel like explaining the way things are with me and Kansas, so I say no. My mom gives me a funny look, but right then JT says that he'll ask her, so I get the job of asking Lefty.

After lunch, I scuffle back out to the barn, not caring if my boots get even dustier than they are. What good are boots if you don't ever get to go on a real ride, anyway? That's what I'd like to know.

Lefty is easy to find. He's in the barn office, sitting at the desk. I explain about the party and ask him if he'll be the voice of the fortune-teller. Talking feels like a lot of work, so I don't use very many words.

"Let me get this straight," he says. "I'm going to tell people I've never even met what's going to happen to them?"

I nod. "Won't even be able to see them, probably."

He twirls a toothpick in his mouth and stares at me. "I've been asked to do some crazy things before, but never anything like this. How'm I supposed to know what's going to happen to them?"

"They are going to be listening to a goat!" I say. "They know it's for fun. Just make the fortunes up."

"You going to help me?"

I shake my head. Making stuff up about people would be fun, except I'm not in a mood for fun. I am only in the mood for a trail ride, and I can't get out of that mood.

"If you change your mind, come find me," he says.

"Okay," I say.

For most of the rest of the afternoon, I wander around in the barn because at least there it feels like I am alone, even if I'm not. And I know things will be crazy in our cabin because the party will be starting in a little while.

I have a pocketful of sugar cubes, so I give them to my favorite horses. I visit Terco first, because I can't help loving her spotty, polka-dotty self, even if she is stubborn. Next I visit Baby Blue, the baby horse that I met right after she was born. But her mother keeps butting in and taking the sugar cubes. Maybe because she doesn't want Baby Blue's teeth to rot and fall out. Or maybe because she wants all the sugar for herself.

My last stop is Twister's stall. When he sees me, he nickers and comes to the stall door. I look around to make sure Kansas isn't coming. Since Twister is being so friendly, I slide open the door and slip into the stall—but I stay right in front of the door so I can get out fast, if I need to. I pat his glossy neck and he blows his breath in my hair, which is different from snorting. I wonder what I was so afraid of on that rainy day when I felt like he had me trapped in there.

I don't say anything to Twister. No one else understands how miserable I am, but somehow Twister does. Maybe he feels just like I do—like no one understands him. We're standing there so peacefully looking into each other's eyes that I can't believe he's wild, like Lefty says. It seems like Twister is getting attached to me, which is even better than Kansas and me being attached. The best thing about animals is that they are warm and furry and you can love them. The next best thing, though, is that they never say mean things. At least not in my language.

. . .

A lot later, after I've given out most of my sugar cubes and patted every single horse, I slump out of the barn. Wrangler Brett catches up to me and asks if I've seen Kansas.

"No," I say. I heave a big sigh.

"You got her figured out yet?"

I shake my head. "Mucked out stalls. Didn't work."

"That rascal! Now she's got you doing her chores? Ah, don't feel bad. Seems like she tries her durnedest to drive everybody away by showing her worst side. I guess she figures that whoever's left after all her antics has earned the right to see how sweet she can be. There aren't too many who can last that long, unfortunately. It just takes time."

"But that's just it! I don't have any more time! Tomorrow is my last chance for a trail ride before the Show-Off. She won't promote me to a trail ride because she hates me!"

"Hold up, there. *Hate*'s a pretty strong word."

I pull myself up straight and tall because I *know* I'm good at words. "It's the right word," I say. "Otherwise, why wouldn't she let me out of that stupid kiddie corral?"

"She must feel like you're not a good enough rider yet. She may be ornery, but she has a good feel for who is ready to go out on the trail and who isn't."

Now my chin goes up, too, all by itself. "This time her feel isn't good. She's wrong because I *am* ready."

Even though we stop talking then, my fighty feelings are still there, making waves at the bottom of my stomach. The waves start out small, and this kind doesn't worry my mom because they aren't very strong. She likes to hear about them before they get bigger, though. Because when the waves get bigger, she says I don't "listen to reason" or even "use good judgment." When my mother says, "You didn't use very good judgment," it means I did something really dumb and maybe even dangerous. So I head back to the cabin to tell her about the waves.

By the time I get there, my parents are getting ready to leave for the party. My mom is in Party Central flittering through all her papers and muttering to herself.

"Mom," I say.

She doesn't look up, but she does say, "Mmmmm?" so I figure there's a forty-three percent chance she's listening.

"You know that thing inside of me that I get sometimes when—"

"Ohhh!" she says, putting her hands on either side of her head like I've just said something really smart. "I bet you're right! It's already inside the bag." She kneels down and digs through her canvas bag and right away pulls out a piece of paper and holds it in the air. "Found it!" she says. But I can't even say "Mom" again before she sticks her nose back in that huge bag and says, "Now if I can just lay my hands on that list. . ."

"Mom, the wave—"

Still looking in the bag, she pats the back of her head. "Oh, I know my hair has a funny wave in the back today. Why I had to have a bad hair day on today of all days, I will never know."

"Remember how you told me I should come talk to you?"

"Here it is!" She checks the watch on her wrist. "Ooo! I have to fly, but I can take a minute to talk. What is it you need?"

A minute is only sixty seconds. Even though I'm really good at fast talking, I know I won't be able to say everything that speedy. And even if I could, there wouldn't be any time left for her to say the right thing so she'd say the *wrong* thing, because the wrong thing is always quicker to say, like "it'll all work out." If my mom said the wrong thing, it would make me feel miles worse. So I just say, "Nothing."

She gives me a quick hug, yells "It's time" at my dad, and then says to me, "I leave you in JT's capable hands."

The waves inside of me slosh around a little harder.

The plan is that JT is the boss of me and Liza for the evening. Oh, joy. For a while, it all goes okay. JT and me watch TV and play "Bet on Baby." It's a game we made up. We each try to guess what Liza will do next—burp, roll over, or cry—and we play to ten. The rules are that the loser changes the next diaper. The score is tied at nine.

"Cry," I say.

JT chews on his thumbnail. We both know that Liza's due to poop any minute, so the stakes are high. "Burp," he says finally.

Liza squirms around a little bit, then squinches up her face, which is turning red. I know that look, and I clap my hands over my ears so I don't have to listen to her scream. But when she opens her mouth, all that comes out is a burp, and then she smiles.

Losing is not my favorite thing to do. "Wait! One more time," I say. "Winner takes all."

"So whoever loses does the diaper *and* dishes?"

"Deal," I say.

Liza has not cried all afternoon. And she always cries when she has to poop, which she is going to have to do any minute. "Cry," I say again.

JT looks down at Liza. Her arms are flailing around. She's still not very good at controlling them, even though she practices all the time. "Nope, I think she's going to smile," he says.

"Smiling isn't a choice. Plus, she hardly ever smiles."

"Then there's a good chance I'll lose."

"But why would you pick that?"

"I don't know. I just have a feeling she will."

Liza doesn't do anything but watch her arms for a long time. If television turns your mind to mush, watching your own arms must turn it to slush, because arms aren't that interesting. Because I'm bored, I finally pick up a teething ring and spin it around my finger. Which makes Liza smile.

"No fair!" I say.

JT grins, which is really annoying.

Luckily for me, the next diaper is only wet, not dirty. JT puts a frozen pizza in the oven and gives Liza her bottle.

Then I burp her. It's kind of fun, the way we all hang out together. The waves in my stomach get smaller, like the kind that just lap at my ankles, and I start feeling a teeny bit better. But then Liza spoils it all by starting to cry. I still think she does it on purpose, even though JT says it's only because she's a baby and that's what babies do.

I escape to my room, closing the door behind me and then putting a pillow over my head. If I lie on my side and arrange the pillow over my head, and put one arm over the pillow, then both ears are covered and I still have one hand free to hold a book and read. The book is about a girl who has her own horse but then it goes lame. The vet fixes the leg, but then the family gets poor, so they put the horse up for sale. And that's as far as I am. Anyway, the book is so good that I get lost in it and pretty soon I don't even hear Liza anymore.

Eventually I notice that it's getting harder and harder to see the words because it's getting dark out. I take the pillow off my head and hear . . . laughing? Yes, laughing. Lots of it. I know JT's laugh, but someone else is laughing, too. I hop out of bed and open the door.

JT is sitting on the floor, leaning over a chessboard, saying, "Right, well, most people call it a 'knight,' even though it does look like a horse, but you can call it whatever you want." Liza is sleeping on the floor next to him and for a minute I wonder if he's talking to her.

But then Kansas, carrying a bowl of pretzels, comes around the corner from the kitchen.

"Oh, hi," she says to me.

"What is *she* doing here?" I say to JT.

"Who, Kansas?" he asks, which proves that JT's thinker really is puny sometimes, because Liza is the only other *she* in the room and I already know what Liza is doing there. "I asked her earlier if she wanted to learn to play chess."

It's bad enough that Kansas spoils horseback riding, but her barging right into my home and right into my life—into my family and my fun night with just JT and Liza—is too much for me.

I spin around in the doorway to my room and slam the door. JT knocks a second later. "G.A.," I say. "I don't want to talk right now."

He comes in anyway, which is really annoying. "What's wrong?"

He asked for it, so I let him have it. "She's like . . . my worst enemy, that's what!"

JT laughs like I'm making a joke. "She is not. She's like your idol. You're always saying, 'Kansas says this, Kansas says that.' You love her."

I stamp my foot. "That was before," I say. "Before she ruined everything and now I can't even get away from her in my own cabin! Why did you have to invite her over?"

"I don't know. I thought tonight might be boring, and—"

"But I would have played chess with you. You could have asked me!"

"I guess I thought that if I taught Kansas to play chess, she might get nicer."

"Why? Why would that make her nicer?"

"Learning something new makes you feel good. At least that's what happened to me when I started running cross-country. And when you feel good, it's easier to be nice."

"But you didn't even ask me whether I cared that she'd be horning in on us!"

"I didn't think it was a big deal. I thought you'd love it."

"I don't. Make her get out."

"Are you crazy? I'm not going to tell her to leave! Besides, she's only here for a little longer. Then she's going to go help out with the party for a while."

"Then I'm leaving."

"No, you're not."

"I'm just going to be in the barn!"

"You can't. Mom's using both walkie-talkies for the fortune-telling, so I won't have any way of keeping track of you."

"I'm nine. I can keep track of myself," I say, thinking that Kansas was right about that walkie-talkie. It does make me feel hobbled.

"Well, I don't, and I'm the one in charge. If you don't want to be around Kansas, just stay in your room."

"Why do you have to be so mean?"

"Why do *you* have to be such a pain?"

"YOU'RE the one who's a PAIN!" I yell, shoving him out the door. Him and me both know that I'm not strong enough to do that unless he wants to be shoved out the door. And I guess this time he does, because all of a sudden he's out and I slam the door. Then, because I feel like it, I open the door and slam it again. I walk back and forth in my room, from the door to the window and back to the door again.

A few days ago, my life was glorious. I had new red cowboy boots, a horse to ride, and Kansas, who I thought would turn into a friend. I had hopes and dreams that were lined up to come true. I think about all the things that have gone *pffft* since then. One: I didn't get to ride—not really. Two: Kansas and I never got attached, like I thought we would. Then tonight, to make things even worse, JT traded her for me. So that's the third thing. Every time I think of a thing, the waves in the bottom of my stomach build bigger and bigger until they are whitecaps, splashing against my chest. At least that's the way it feels. Four: I lost at "Bet on Baby." Five: I have to stay in this stupid room. Six—

But then, as I turn around at the window, I think about the fifth thing again. *I have to stay in this stupid room.* Which is annoying because it's not fair. Everyone else is out having fun and I'm stuck here. I hate it when I don't have any choices, when I can't do anything or change anything. I'm locked up, like a prisoner.

Except that . . . I'm not. Not really.

10. Breaking Away

It isn't hard to do, once I think of it. The waves inside of me have an undertow that suck me right into what comes next. Which is, I break out of there and make things happen, all on my own.

All the rooms in the cabin are on the first floor, so I just open the window and climb out. I scrape my cheek on the windowsill, but I don't care. I'm excited to be out, free, and *away* from everyone making me feel bad. When I get to the barn, Twister's staring out his window at the woods and the hills. I bet he feels locked up, too. I know just what to do.

All day I've been thinking about my problems. I'm sick of thinking and . . . and *I'm not going to do it anymore!* I sprint down to the tack room and grab the bridle off the hook that says TWISTER above it. His saddle is there, too, but I leave it. It's too heavy for me. When I get back to Twister, I feed him a sugar cube to remind him that we're friends now. While he's crunching it down, I get the bit in his mouth and slip the bridle over his ears. I've watched the wranglers do it lots of times. I fasten the strap and lead him out the back of the barn.

Next I look for a leg up. A way to get on Twister so we can both get away from being cooped up and ruled in and hobbled. I climb onto a wagon that the ranch uses for hayrides and try to lead Twister so he's right beside it. He shakes his head. I hold out another sugar cube. He steps just where I need him to. In the next second, I slide onto his back.

I'm on!

Outside the kiddie corral. Without Kansas or Lefty or anyone. Just me.

For a minute, Twister stands completely still. Then something about him changes. I lean forward a little and grab hold of a big bunch of his wiry mane. And an amazing thing happens. He starts to walk. I put the reins on his neck and ask him to turn onto the trail that leads into the woods. He does. My balance is good. I'm not going to fall. I take a deep breath and breathe in the fresh air of happiness. This is what I wanted all along. I knew I could do it! There's a part of me that wants to shout out, *See? I told you so!* But it's impossible to talk because my mouth is stuck in a big smile.

There's another part of me that's whispering, *You are going to be in so much trouble*, but I'm not listening to that part. This trail ride on Twister, by myself, is worth any consequences my parents can think of. Instead of listening to the part of me that's worried, I listen to the *thud, thud,*

thud of Twister's hooves on the trail. It's very quiet, like the woods is holding its breath.

The sun is going down, and already the woods is full of shadows. Twister's neck is arched and his ears are pricked straight up. I can tell by the way he's watching everything that he's as happy to be out here as I am. If he could talk, he'd say, *Thank you, Mary Margaret, for breaking me free and riding me so gently and so well. You are a natural at riding. Kansas was being a jerk.* Well, maybe he wouldn't have said that last thing about Kansas, since they are a team, but it's fun to pretend.

I think of how I probably look up there on him. I must look like a real wrangler, now that my boots are dirty and I'm out on the trail, on a real horse that doesn't have all kinds of dumb ideas, like Terco does. I feel a little guilty for a second, thinking bad about Terco, who was the first horse love of my life. But now I'm ready for bigger things. I'm ready for—

But right in the middle of that thought, I hear a branch snap in the woods, and Twister shies to the left. Out of the corner of my eye, I see a flick of white, and that's the last thing I see before our escape gets rough and wild.

My hands grab onto Twister's mane all on their own, like they know what's going to happen before my brain does. Twister shoots out from underneath me. For a second, it's like I'm sitting on only air. Then I feel a yank on my arms and after that I'm sort of back on Twister, but bouncing and jouncing all over the place. Somehow I hold on. Which is not easy to do when the horse is at a flat-out run and it feels like you left your brains in a lump somewhere behind you on the trail. And it's hard to think without a brain.

"Wah, wah, wah—*whoa*," I cry.

Maybe I shouldn't have said anything! Now Twister will know from my shaky voice that I'm scared. More scared than when I went through the haunted house with JT before I knew all the blood on the monsters was just ketchup and the bones in the coffins were plastic. That night I could pretend to be brave because JT was holding my hand and I knew that the haunted house had a door. Once we were outside, everything would be all right. But JT isn't here. There isn't a way out. Or even any brakes.

I look down and see the reins are still in my hands. Too bad I can't use them. I am too busy holding on. Twister's mane is whipping at my face and my eyes. Everything blurs by me in big chunks of green and brown.

I hang on for as long as Twister stays on the trail—all the way through the woods, then through a big field, and around a lake. That's when he jags off the trail and I can't tell anymore which direction he'll turn. I close my eyes, cling to his neck, and have a little talk with God. "Please make Twister stop so I can get off. I'll change all Liza's dirty diapers, write thank-you notes before Mom bugs me to, and stop snooping in JT's life."

I open my eyes in time to see that we're coming to a stream. Twister slows down. Maybe he'll stop because of the stream. Instead, his running gets choppy. He's not going to stop at all. *He's going to jump it!*

By the time I think it, he's doing it. I open my mouth and "Wah—ay—eeee!" comes out. There's a flash of blue under me and a thud when we land on the other side of the stream. Then there's another thud.

It is the thud of me, landing flat on my back.

I lay there for a second, looking up at the dusky sky. Something is wrong, but I don't know what. In the second second, I *do* know what. My body isn't doing its job of breathing. I want to suck in some air, but I can't. Instead, all the breath is being pressed out of me.

Eh-h-h-h-h-h.

It seems like my chest is made out of rock instead of out of blood and guts and lungs, which is what normal chests have.

Eh-h-h-h-h.

Here I am, out in the country. Alone. Practically dead. In another minute, I will be all the way dead. Everyone is going to be sorry—especially Kansas. This is all her fault. If she would have let me go on a trail ride none of this would have happened! Serves her right that I'm going to be dead. I hope she goes to jail. Then she'll see what it's like to want to ride and not be able to. Yeah, I can't wait to see that. But then I remember that I'll be dead, so I won't actually be around to see that. I still hope she goes to jail.

Suddenly my breath rushes back into me, and I can breathe again. Just like that, I'm not going to die, which is maybe a little bit disappointing because Kansas won't get thrown in jail. But also glorious because I like being alive.

I lie there and breathe and breathe and breathe. And then I cry because I'm not going to die and because the ride on Twister was wild and scary. And because I don't know what I should do next.

I thought that I could handle anything on the Lazy K Ranch. Also, I thought I could handle Twister. Too bad it turns out I'm not good at either of those things. I don't know where I am. Or how I'll get back. Or if there are coyotes or bears watching me from the woods, thinking that I look like a Happy Meal.

The sun is down and the skylight is getting dark, but it's still light enough that I can see Twister grazing a little ways from me.

A baby vulture dips and flits above me. He must think I look yummy. I wave my arms at him. "Look! They're scrawny!" I shout. "No meat on them!" I'm still crying, so my words come out start-and-stop.

But all that does is scare Twister even farther away.

Finally I stand up and brush myself off. Everything feels scraped or bruised, like I'm one big sore, but at least my arms and legs are still working. I don't know what to do next, so I limp toward Twister. He watches me until I get close, then trots a few steps away.

"Come on, boy," I say. My voice still sounds slurpy with tears and snot. "Let's just hang out together so maybe the vultures and coyotes will leave us alone." I pat my pockets, looking for a sugar cube, but they're gone. He keeps watching me, walking away from me every time I walk toward him. Finally, I sit down next to a big rock and hope that he won't leave me all alone. Out here in the wilderness. In the very darkest dark, which it's going to be soon.

I think about my mom and how we sometimes still play "What if?" It's a game she made up when I was little to make sure I'd know what to do if something bad happened. She'll say, "What if a stranger tries to pull you into a car on the street?" I answer, "I kick, bite, and shout, 'This man is not my parent!'" Sometimes I make up funny answers to her questions. Once she asked me, "What if the milk smells sour?" I know the answer is to pour it down the drain and add "milk" to the grocery list, but once I said, "I feed it to Liza." She didn't think it was funny, but JT thought it was hilarious! Anyway, because of the game, I remember that the answer to "What if you get lost?" is "Stay in one place" because it's easier to get found that way.

But what if no one is even looking? JT usually just ignores me when I'm crabby, which I was when he came to my room back at the cabin. He probably still thinks I'm pouting in my room, and he's having so much *fun* playing chess with Kansas, he'll never notice I'm gone. He doesn't care about me, anyway. Mom and Dad are at the party and won't be back until late. No one saw me leave. No one knows I'm gone. Which means no one's missing me—and that might be the worst thing of all.

It seems like I'm there for a long time. The air is getting colder. I wish I'd worn a jacket. But I didn't think about that when I ran away. I didn't think about anything but just getting away from there. Now all I want to do is get back.

The first star comes out. Even though I am too big to believe a star can make a wish come true, I whisper the words my grandpa and I say every time I stay overnight at the farm.

Star light, star bright,
First star I see tonight.
I wish I may, I wish I might,
Have the wish I wish tonight.

I squeeze my eyes closed and wish the biggest wish of my life. I wish that Liza will poop. If she does, JT will have to go into my bedroom to get a diaper. And then he will see that I'm gone.

I listen to the trickle of the stream. *Who who-whoo?* goes an owl. And I wonder the same thing. Who, who, who will find me? I listen to Twister crunching on grass. After a while, I try to sneak up on him but he sees me and trots in a big circle. I was right about one thing: he sure likes being free. Even though I know I'll never catch him, I run after him. I don't know what else to do and I have to do something.

At first I think the thrumming I hear is just my heart.

But the sound keeps getting louder, even when I stop running, and then I see a light flickering through the trees. The light comes out into the field, and I know it's the quad. Someone is coming for me on the quad! The headlights bob up and down across the field.

"Over here! Over here!" I shout, climbing up onto the rock. "Here I am!"

Suddenly the lights stop bobbing and a spotlight is blinding me. "Mary Margaret?" a voice yells.

I squint into the light. "JT?"

"I'll be right there!" he shouts. The quad bumps across the field and through the stream. It's almost to me when it bounces through a hole and stops again. Then I don't hear the sound of the engine at all, only JT saying, "Rat butt! Now what?"

I run over to him as quick as I can. He's still sitting in the seat when I get there. I throw my arms around his head and squeeze. "I know I'm not supposed to be here but Twister got spooked and all I could do was hang on and I couldn't stop him but I stayed on him for a long time even though he was galloping through the woods and trees and everything but after a while my arms were so tired and then he jumped the stream and I fell and I thought I was going to die again because there wasn't any breath left in my body but then I didn't die at least not that way but then I saw that I was lost and then there were coyotes and bears and vultures to be afraid of and, oh JT, you're my hero! If it weren't for you, I'd be dead!"

"You're okay," he says, almost to himself. He hugs me back for a second and then says, "The hug is from Mom, because I know she'd want me to hug you." Then he lets go of me and slugs me in the arm. "And that's from me because what you did was so stupid."

"Ouch! JT, that really hurt."

"You're in so much trouble!"

"So Mom and Dad know what I did?"

"Not yet. They left me in charge, Mary Missing-in-Action. That means I'm responsible for you. I'm in so much trouble. *You're* in so much trouble!"

"Stop saying that!"

"Okay, but you are."

"Oh, I don't care," I say, throwing my arms around his head again and squeezing tight. "Anything is better than being eaten by coyotes, or vultures. I really did see one flittering around, a baby one."

"If it was flittering, it was probably a bat," he mumbles into my arm, trying to squirm away. "Get off of me already. I think this thing is broken."

I let him go. "The quad? What happened?"

"I don't know. Here. Hold the flashlight and shine it right down on the steering wheel." I do what he tells me. He turns the key a couple of times but nothing happens.

JT leans back in the seat and crosses his arms. "I don't know what to do with this thing. Let's get the horse. Where is he?"

"Grazing over there. I tried to catch him."

"It'll be easier with two of us," he says, getting off the quad.

I follow JT toward Twister. "Then what?"

"We'll lead him back. I have a flashlight and I know where we are. I've been running back here almost every day. If we're lucky, we'll get there before Kansas has to explain to Mom and Dad why she's watching Liza instead of me."

"Oh," I say. No wonder he punched me. First he lost me and then he had to leave Liza because of me. "How did you find out I was gone?"

"After Kansas left for the party, I went in to see if you were okay."

"You did? Even though I was crabby?"

"Yes. What did you think? I wouldn't just leave you there to rot."

Those words—*I wouldn't just leave you there to rot*—make me feel warm on the inside even though I'm cold on the outside. "Thanks," I say.

He shakes his head like I'm strange, but I don't care.

I keep that warm feeling the whole time we chase Twister around the field and through the stream, trying to catch him. It lasts until the second that JT, while kind of leaping for the reins, falls. I don't see it happen because it's completely dark out. All I see is the light from the flashlight go down at the same time that I hear a thud. Then JT says a bad word, which I've never heard him do before.

I run over there, pick up the flashlight, and shine it into

his face. His mouth and eyes are all squinched up like he's really hurt, but at least he's got Twister's reins, and that's a happiness.

"Get the light out of my face!" he says.

"What are you yelling at me for? It's not my fault you fell!" I say. What I'm thinking is, Please don't be hurt bad. It's like what I want to say gets lost on the way to my mouth, and then my mouth just makes something up to say because that's what mouths do—they talk.

"Get a clue! *All* of this is your fault! Twister, the quad, and now . . . ow!"

That warm feeling I had about me and JT turns icy. Things don't look so good for us right then. Out in the country. In the dark. With JT really hurt. And no way home.

I help JT try to stand up, but he can't. "All you have to do is keep your foot stiff," I say.

He crumbles back onto the ground. "If I *could*, I *would*." His face is white and he's biting his lip. He rolls down his sock to look at his ankle. It's already starting to swell up. Pretty soon it's going to be as big as those grapefruits that my aunt Wendie sends my mom every Christmas.

"Does it hurt much?"

He groans and lies back on the grass. "Yeah, it does. I think I'm going to pass out. You have to go get help . . ." He holds out the reins to me. "Ride Twister back to those trees." He stops, like he has to rest from talking.

"JT?"

He takes a big breath. "I'll be okay. Just . . . follow the

tree line. It leads right to the trail. Take the trail back to the ranch."

"You mean . . . leave you here? And me go—by myself, through the woods and everything?"

He nods.

In the light from the flashlight, I look at Twister, who is looking at me. I'm pretty sure he's holding a grudge. My insides feel like pudding, just thinking about doing it. But I try to think about how I have to do it for JT. He needs me, so I will do it.

While I lead Twister over to the quad and climb up on it, I can't stop thinking about what it was like, Twister running away with me and not being able to get off or stop him, and not knowing when or how he'd stop. I couldn't do anything. It was like I was . . . nothing, at least to Twister.

I swallow hard. I put the reins over his neck again and get ready to swing my leg over his back. But my leg doesn't cooperate. It stays stuck right to the quad.

"Wait a minute," I yell.

"What?"

"It's just . . . I don't think this is a very good plan."

"You don't like the plan," JT mumbles. I can hardly hear him.

"It just seems like we should stay together." I shine the flashlight over the field to where I know he's lying. I can see he's on his side and his knees are folded up close to his chin. He says, like he's tired, "For once, can you not talk something to death and just do it?"

"Don't worry. I'll get help. I promise." I mean it when I say it. I will get help for him. I just don't know how yet. "Maybe we could just wait here until help comes."

JT does a grunt-laugh. "Uh, no. Everyone's still at the party."

I'm still standing on the quad. "What about the quad?"

"It's broken."

I scramble off it and hand JT the reins. "Here, hold Twister. I'm going to try the key again. Maybe the engine just needed a rest."

I turn the key. Nothing happens.

"It's not like a computer," says JT. "You can't fix it just by turning it back on."

I clunk my forehead onto the steering handle and just stay like that, with my arms dangling down. What are we going to do?

I hear Twister breathing and JT groans a little, but otherwise it's quiet, which is good for thinking. And when my right hand bumps into something by accident, my brain twitches. I remember Lefty fixing something down there, and complaining about wranglers riding it too hard, like it was a toy. What was it he said he was fixing? Something that reminded me of fire or flicker . . . no, but something like that . . . sparkle . . .

And then I've got it!

"Spark plugs!" I say. "It might be the spark plugs!"

JT doesn't look happy, which I thought he would. "Right," he says. "Now you're a mechanic. That'll come in handy when you have to help me with the prosthetic leg I'm going to need if I don't get help soon."

"No, I remember now. Lefty was fixing them one day and complaining about the wranglers riding it too hard. I was handing him the tools."

"If you'd just gotten on that stupid horse when I asked you to, you'd be at the ranch by now getting help. Why can't you just—"

"Because my way is better! If I'm right, we can both go together."

JT starts to say something but before he can, I open the box that's strapped behind the seat and find the right wrench—the one I called a baby wrench. "I'll hold the flashlight. You fix it."

"This is dumb! I don't know anything about engines," JT says, but he lets me help him up. He bends his knee so that his hurt ankle isn't touching the ground, and then he leans on me and uses me as his good leg.

It's a good thing that JT figures out what to do with the spark plugs. Because my only other idea for getting out of there was that I be his good leg all the way back to the ranch. I would have done it, too, because JT's my brother, and I would do anything for him, almost. It works out best for both of us that he fixes the quad.

Once we figure that out, the rest of rescuing ourselves is easy. The controls for stopping and going are all on the handles, so JT doesn't have to use his feet at all. We go kind of slow, trying not to hit any bumps because bumping around makes JT's foot hurt worse.

We drive back to the ranch on the trail, me holding the reins and Twister trotting along behind us. I think about how glorious riding Twister was at first, and how good it felt to know that Kansas was wrong about me. But when Twister ran away with me, straight away from my problems just like I wanted, it wasn't glorious at all. It was scary. I was afraid I'd fall, die (and I almost did, according to me), and get eaten. And I was scared I wouldn't be able to get back to my mom and dad and JT. Because if I couldn't get back, what would happen to my room and all my books and toys and even Hershey?

Liza would get them! And (now that I am safe and almost home) that thought is scarier than all the other scary things put together.

Here are the things I have to do because I sneaked out last night, didn't have my walkie-talkie (which wasn't my fault, since they were using it for the party), rode away on Twister without asking or even telling anyone, almost got killed, made JT leave Liza, turned JT into a criminal because he had to take the quad to find me, which is against the law for thirteen-year-olds. And because I got JT seriously wounded.

1. All of JT's chores until he can do them himself.
2. Five hours of community service, which Mom and Dad say doesn't pay back for how I turned JT into a criminal but at least it's a start.
3. Apologize to Kansas. Which is the worst thing of all because it was her fault that all that other stuff was my fault.

Here are the things I can't do because I sneaked out last night, didn't have my walkie-talkie (which wasn't my fault, since they were using it for the party), rode away on Twister without asking or even telling anyone, almost got killed, made JT leave Liza, turned JT into a criminal because he had to take the quad to find me, which is against the law for thirteen-year-olds. And because I got JT seriously wounded.

1. Go to my friend Ellie's sleepover.
2. Watch TV or play games on the computer for two weeks. Good thing I like to read.
3. Speak to JT—ever again. (JT added that one. He's still a little mad.)

I think I should get extra credit for figuring out how to get home, but everyone is obsessed with how it was me who got us into that whole situation, not how it was me who got us out.

"I bet number four is going to be that I can't ride again, right?" I say.

My parents look at each other. My mom arches an eyebrow at my dad, which means . . . I'm not sure what it means. I only know that they are talking to each other without using any words.

"No," they say at the same time.

"No? You mean I can ride again?"

"Yes," my mom says. "You can ride again."

"You mean like in another year or when I get to be a grown-up, right?"

"No, you can ride again now," my dad says.

"Right now? Here?"

"Yes," says my mom. My mom's and dad's eyes are straight on me, like they are trying to figure something out about me. "We talked to Lefty about it this morning. We thought you should lose riding privileges. Lefty thought about it and even discussed it with Kansas. He said that after a harrowing experience like the one you had, if you didn't get back on a horse here, you might never try it again. He wants you to ride." And then she and my dad add, at the very same second, *"With supervision."*

"Another session in the corral, and you'll be good to go for the show," says my dad.

The Rider Show-Off! To win it tomorrow, I will have to get on a horse. Which I don't want to think about. I decide I am all talked out on the particular subject of horses. I find a new one.

"How was the party?" I ask. "Did everybody like Goose?"

My dad tilts his head back and laughs. "Like him?" he says. "They took to him like—what was it that Lefty said, Lil? 'They took to him like sick kittens to a warm brick!'"

"The Bearded Wonder was definitely a hit," says my mom. "Once in a while he'd snag a roll or some green beans off a guest's plate, but no one seemed to care."

"That's because the food wasn't that good," my dad says, winking at me.

My mother ignores him. "It was terrific food, and terrific fun. They want to do the whole thing again next year, only in Hawaii, and they want me to bring the Bearded Wonder along."

"Look out," says my dad. "Goose'll eat the grass skirt off every guest!"

"Can we come to Hawaii, too?" I ask my mom. "Please, oh please, oh please!" Already I can see myself swimming with the dolphins and surfing with the sharks.

My mom raises an eyebrow at me. "Missy," she says. "I don't think now's the best time to ask that, after what you did last night."

Shoot! I think. How did we get back on that subject? "Oh yeah," I say.

"Oh yeah," she says. "Why don't you go meet up with Kansas in the corral and practice for the Rider Show-Off?"

"After last night, Kansas will never let me ride in that thing."

"It was Kansas's idea, as a matter of fact," says my mom. "She said to meet her there right about now and she'll help you with Terco."

I rub my hand up and down my side. "I don't know. I'm still pretty sore." I touch the Band-Aids on my face. "And scraped up. It'd probably be best to wait. Yeah, I'll wait."

"Hmm," goes my mom. "Maybe you'll feel differently once you get to the corral. Why don't you just go out there and see? Besides, it'll be a good chance to tell Kansas you're sorry."

I don't really feel like being around Kansas or apologizing to her. I don't even feel like being around horses.

But because I'm already in a bundle of trouble, I do what my mom says.

Terco is tied up to the corral; it looks like she's just waiting for me. Kansas is giving Bob the hose treatment outside the corral, rubbing the hose between his ears. I don't say anything for a long time, which is hard for me, but not as hard as saying I'm sorry to Kansas. Finally, all the other stuff I want to talk about builds up in me, but I know I better say I'm sorry first, because otherwise I might not get around to it.

"I'm sorry I took Twister," I say.

"It was a dumb thing to do," she says. Bob butts his head up against her chest. He doesn't even notice the hose anymore.

"I know."

"Then why'd you do it?"

I shrug.

"Well, it was stupid."

"I already said I know. Why do you have to be so mean about it?"

"Because real horses aren't like merry-go-round horses," she says. "They aren't just pretty toys."

"All I wanted was to go on a trail ride."

"But you have to be ready for it first. You would have known that if you were any good at listening, because we were all telling you that."

Just then I think of something, and it's a big something. I put my hands on my hips. "If I'm so bad at listening, then how come I remembered what Lefty said about the spark plugs, huh?"

"Well, you—" But then she stops. "Okay, you're right. You did listen that time, which proves that you can, when you want to. Maybe you could just listen a little more instead of being so bullheaded about stuff and wanting everything to be your way or the highway."

"What's that mean?"

"That everything had to be exactly the way you wanted it. You just *had* to go on a trail ride, so JT got hurt. And you and Twister could have been."

Even though my mom and dad have been saying exactly the same thing, hearing Kansas say it is different. Harder.

I gulp. "I'm sorry," I say again. Only this time I'm not just saying the words. I feel sorry. "Is Twister—?"

"He's okay—he looks a lot better'n you or your brother, that's for sure. He's taking it easy in his stall."

I heave a big sigh of relief. "I won't be taking it easy again until I'm at least twelve. You should see all the stuff my parents are making me do."

She must feel sorry for me, because she suddenly starts being nicer to me. "Horses, especially jittery ones like Twister, spook all the time. It sounds like you rode tough for a long time. JT says you made it all the way to the creek in the back meadow."

"Only because I couldn't get him to stop."

She drops the hose and gives Bob a pat on the withers.

"Good boy, Bob." Then she says to me, "You want to give Terco another try?"

"Not right now. I'm—I'm still kind of sore," I say, rubbing my back. "You know, from the fall and all."

She squinches up her eyes at me. "Sure," she says. "I know. But you'll still ride in the Show-Off, right?"

"You bet!" I say. Then I skally-hoot myself right out of there, before she can ask me any more questions.

Friday is a sunny, cool day that's perfect for the Rider Show-Off. My mom calls it crisp, but I call it glorious. We all sit on the bottom row of the bleachers so that Liza can sit in her stroller and JT can rest his sore foot on the bottom rung of the fence around the corral.

"Up next is Jus-tin Swan-son!" says the announcer, very dramatic. "Go get 'em, Justin!" My stomach does flippety-flops every time I think about riding, so I don't watch Justin "go get 'em."

I look past the corral and into the pasture. I grin big at what I see there. It's Baby Blue, just running and hopping and bucking all over the place. If she could talk she'd be yelling, "Hey! Watch what I can do!" And she'd probably buck around some. Then she'd shout, "You think that was good? Watch this!" And then she'd run and buck *and* twist—all at the same time. JT would say she's being *obnoxious* but I just think she's full of high spirits.

"Kara Kazinski on Deronda," the announcer blares. I hear Deronda's pounding hooves, but I keep my eyes on

Baby Blue. It seems like just yesterday she was a baby, with her hair all matted from being born, but it's already been a few days! I think about how, because I rubbed her so good, now she knows she can trust skinny, two-legged things like me and Lefty and Kansas. I remember how she kept falling when she tried to stand up, and how I was afraid she was going to give up but she didn't because she couldn't. It was just like Lefty said—quitting wasn't in her nature. She kept scrabbling up every time she fell down. If she'd quit, she wouldn't be out there, rearing and twisting and bucking sideways and making her own fun.

"Nice job, Kara! Way to make Deronda turn on a dime and give you fifteen cents back in change. That's the way it's done, folks. Give her a hand." The announcer didn't even need to say that last part, since everyone already *is* giving her a hand. "We're going to take a little break so our next group of riders can get ready. Next up is Mary Margaret, then Nicole."

Suddenly I think that I'm really not going to be able to do it. I look over at Kansas. She's standing next to Terco, holding her reins, and motioning me to *come on!* I scuffle over there, not even worrying about my boots. I pat Terco, trying to up-talk myself into getting on, but when I smell that sweet horsey smell and feel the wiry mane, that ride on Twister fills up my memory and the butterflies in my stomach start to panic. And then I do, too.

"I can't!" I say to Kansas. "I—I'm *allergic!*"

"To horses? Since when?"

"It came on suddenly. This morning!" I don't want any-one to know I'm scared, especially Kansas, but it's like she's listening to my thoughts instead of my words.

"It won't be like it was on Twister," she says. "Remember, this is Terco—the horse that's barely alive."

"Riders ready?" says the announcer. Kansas gives him the thumbs-up.

"No, riders are *not* ready," I snip at Kansas. I look down at my boots and wish I was Kansas instead of me. I wait for her to say something mean about how dumb it is for me to be scared.

Instead she says, "Tell you what. We'll make a deal. You do this for me now and I'll do something for you later—whatever you want. Come on. You can do this, if you set your mind to it. I know you can, and I'm always right."

She might be able to listen to my thoughts, but Kansas can't see all the way inside me. She can't see I'm too scared to make that deal. I don't say anything.

In the pasture, Baby Blue is kicking up her heels again. Suddenly, she slides to a stop, lowers her head, and looks right at me like she's saying, *Now* you! *It's your turn to show what you're made of. Or are you going to be a quitter and miss out on all the fun?*

That does it. I don't care if people think I'm a quitter, but to have a horse who is younger than I am think that about me? No, ma'am!

"Okay," I say. Kansas grins and puts her hands together so they make a stirrup for me. She lifts me up and up and

I swing my leg over and then I'm on, all the way on Terco, and it's not scary—or at least not as scary as I thought it would be. Terco's back is wide and solid. I hold the saddle horn for a second, just to make sure it's there.

"Show her who's boss," says Kansas.

I boot Terco to show her I mean business and she turns into the ring.

All the other kids knew where they were supposed to make their horse go, like in a figure eight or all the way to the end around the barrel. But I decide to just make it all up. When I ride past the announcer, I stick out my arm for the microphone, like I know exactly what I'm doing. He is so surprised that he hands it over. I pronunciate into the microphone, "MARY MARGARET ANDERSON COMING TO YOU FROM HIGH ATOP TERCO!" It comes out so loud over the loudspeaker that everyone puts their hands over their ears.

"Ooops," I say. "Sorry about that." And then I say, "Also, just so you know, it's okay to clap for me now." And everyone does.

Terco is still stubborn, but I think that the wild ride on Twister made me stronger because I can make her go where I want, mostly. Well, about half the time. We compromise. I get her to go in one direction for a few steps and then she goes in the opposite direction for a few steps before I can get her to go back in the direction I want to go in again. What it looks like, though, is that we are zigzagging on purpose all the way down to the end of the corral.

It's not the trail ride that I've been dreaming of, but after that ride on Twister, I kind of had enough of trail riding anyway.

The best part is that on the way back, I get Terco to do something I bet she's never done before. I make her trot! She and I both know the only reason she's letting me "make" her is because she's heading back toward the barn. But she can't talk, and I'll never tell. Even though I'm not cantering around the corral, being back on Terco feels like a glory to me. A quiet one, but still a glory.

After my turn, when I get off Terco, Kansas gives me a big hug. I am so surprised that the words *Want to come for a sleepover tonight?* sneak right out of me. Kansas is still wedged in my heart. She ruined everything for me and I stole her horse and then she helped me get back on a horse. She is *Kansas*, and more than anything I still want her to like me.

"Okay," she says. I don't know if that word sneaked out of her or if she meant to say it, and I don't even care.

"There. I think that's everything," says Kansas later that night, scratching something off the list of fun things I wanted us to do together. I wrote the list as soon as my mom said that yes, Kansas could come for a sleepover.

Kansas tosses the list and the pencil onto my bed.

I pick up the list. "We've played miniature golf, made grilled-cheese sandwiches, watched cartoons, and you took me on a trail ride on the back of Terco. We've said good-bye to my favorite horses, including kissing their soft noses."

Kansas holds up her finger. "*And* I introduced you to everyone—even to people who already know you, including JT and your mom and dad—as 'this is my new friend, Mary Margaret,' just like you wanted. Is there anything else? When I made that deal with you at the Rider Show-Off I didn't know what I was in for."

I put the eraser to my chin. "Give me a minute," I say.

It's easy for me to do two things at once, so while I'm thinking about that I say, "Why are you named after a state? I mean, I like your name and everything, but I've never known someone named after a state."

"I'll tell you, but you have to swear on the wild mustang grave that you won't tell."

I hold my right hand up and say, all serious, "I swear," even though I've never heard of the wild mustang grave.

"My real name's Kate."

I have a lot to say about that, like how I know five Kates, Cates, and Caits, and even a Qate. And how I think "Kate" sounds a little like a cough when you say it. But I know that too much talking ruins things with Kansas. So I just say, "Really?"

"When I was nine, I decided it was too plain. And the word *plain* made me think of the plains, and then I thought of Kansas and now that's who I am."

"Can you do that? Just change your name?" Already I am thinking about all the names I could have. Anastasia or

Ralaykeyshonna, which I just made up, or Pomeranian, which is a breed of dog I like but which might be too fru-fru for a girl like me.

"I don't know, but I did," she says.

We both sit there thinking for a minute. I am keeping my lips pressed very tightly together so all the stuff I'm thinking doesn't spill out and annoy Kansas. Which is just about killing me.

Finally, I let just a few words dribble out. "If it isn't legal, that would make you an outlaw, sort of."

Kansas grins and nods. "Yeah, and how cool is that?"

Then she says even more, maybe because she has a chance while I'm still not talking much. "Getting back on Terco again wasn't so bad, was it?"

"No. I was scared. I know you thought I could do it, but I didn't think I could."

"I told you I'm always right."

"Yeah, but so am I."

I lie down and dangle my head and arms off the edge of the bed near Kansas, who's sitting on her sleeping bag.

"Kansas?" I say.

"What?"

I try to pack everything I want to say into just a few words. "What about this? Was this so bad?"

"What—hanging out with you?"

I nod. I've been having fun, but if you're really friends then both people have fun when you hang out.

She has a funny smile on her face. "Nah, it isn't bad at

all. Even though you can be way more annoying than me, you and me are a lot alike. Nobody can make either of us do anything we don't want to do. Ever."

I throw my arms around her and give her a monster squeeze. She lets me for a minute.

"Kansas?" I ask, after I let her wriggle out of my hug.

"Yeah?"

"Well . . . it's just that . . . what took you so long to like me?"

"Lots of people who come up here are, I don't know, snobs. They think they're better than me. When you couldn't believe that I didn't have a computer, I thought that's what you were—a snob. So I guess after that I was just set on not liking you. And then you and JT did that stupid thing with Goose. And all your talking kind of gets in the way, which you know."

"All I wanted was to be friends."

"Yeah, that's what JT said, too, later. All that stuff you did, though—I just took it all wrong."

"We're okay now, though." I don't ask it. I say it because I know it's a fact.

"Yeah, we're okay now." She points to the list. "But are we square? Have we done everything you wanted to?"

I start to say yes, but then she tucks her hair behind her ear and all three of her earrings shine in the light. Suddenly I know that there's just one more thing I have to have before I leave the Lazy K Ranch. "Almost square," I say.

"What else?"

I lean forward and whisper it to her.

She puts her hand over her mouth and laughs. "*What?!* Aren't you already in enough trouble?"

"Please?" I beg. "Just one hole in one ear. That's all! I'll keep my hair over it until we get home so you won't get in trouble. Please?"

"It's going to hurt, though."

"I don't care. I really want to."

"Boy, we're even more alike than I thought," she says, pulling the silver horseshoe earring out of her ear. "I'll give you this one because you're going to need all the luck you can get!"

This time it takes her longer to escape my hugging arms. "Thanks, Kansas! This is going to be so cool!"

"I need rubbing alcohol, a needle, and a plastic baggy of ice," she says. She shakes her head like she isn't so sure about this.

"I know right where to find them," I say, hopping up to get them before she can change her mind.

Too bad for me that I run smack into my mom on my way back to my room. "Mary Margaret, what've you got there?"

"Oh, just . . . " And then I realize that I am out of practice at talking. And while I try to find words to say next, she sees the bottle of rubbing alcohol, which JT sometimes uses on his face. She also sees the needle and the baggy of ice. And then I guess she does some math in her brain. Rubbing alcohol + needle + ice = pierced ears.

"No," she says, taking the stuff out of my hands. "I can't even believe you're thinking of it! One of my friends did that when we were kids and she got an infection and her earlobe ballooned up like a cherry tomato!"

"But, Mom—"

"Absolutely not. End of discussion."

That's why I don't get my ear pierced after all. But Kansas lets me keep the horseshoe earring anyway.

The next day, we pack up to leave. I have to help twice as much because JT can't help at all. And when I try to complain about it, nobody listens.

"Not. One. Word," says my mother, handing me another bag to carry out to the van.

JT smirks. "I did your unloading when we got here, so it's only fair that you do my loading now. If it weren't for you, I wouldn't even be—"

"—on these stinking crutches," I finish for him. He has told me that about a million times in the last two days. *Ugh.* Brothers! Even Liza is scowling at me. *Ugh.* Babies!

When the last suitcase is finally smooshed into the back and Liza is strapped into her car seat, where she belongs (all the time, if it was up to me), I suddenly remember something.

I trot my red boots toward the barn.

"Mary Margaret!" yells my dad. "We're leaving!"

"I forgot to say good-bye to Lefty and Wrangler Brett! I'll be right back!"

I hear JT groan, "It figures," but I keep going.

Wrangler Brett and Lefty are standing outside Twister's stall.

"This is the end of the trail for me," I say to them. "We have to go home now."

"*Hasta luego,*" Wrangler Brett says, shaking my hand. "Don't let anybody push you around." He laughs like he's cracked a joke.

"I won't. Bye, Lefty. Thanks for everything."

Lefty just looks at me for a minute. "You thinkin' bout coming back here ever?" he finally says.

"You bet!"

"Be sure to give me ample warning so I can clear out," he says, winking at me. Then he gives me a cowboy hug, which is really a half hug because he only uses one arm. But it feels good anyway.

I turn toward the stalls, where all the horses are eating, throw out my arms, and say, "Good-bye, horses!" And then I skally-hoot right out of there and all the way to the van, where everyone is waiting for me, just like always.

Because I am worth waiting for.

13. What I Got Out of It

On the Monday after spring break, Mr. Mooney, who wants every speck of our lives to be a "learning experience," makes us all write a report about what we got out of spring break. Mine goes like this.

What I Got Out of My Spring Break
by Me! (Mary Margaret)

Here are the things I got out of my spring break. I got *out of town* (get it??? Ha ha!) because my mom had to plan this big party where a goat named Goose told people what was going to happen to them next. I wasn't there, but my friend Kansas told me that the guests really believed what Goose said!

I got red cowboy boots that were clean and new when we left and dirty and old when we came back. I still like them just as much and maybe even better.

I got a horseshoe earring from my friend

Kansas. She says the earring works great as a pin, so I wear it on my collar. (I'm wearing it today. Did you notice?)

What else did I get? Oh! I got some new ways of saying things, like "tongue oil." If you say somebody's got tongue oil it means they talk a lot. My friend Kansas told me it was a good expression for me to know. On her advice, I used a little less tongue oil for a whole day, and talked less. Don't worry, though. It's not permanent. And if you say someone has "taken some hair off the dog," it means she got experience doing something the hard way.

But what I *almost* got out of my spring break is more exciting than what I did get. I almost got killed three times. Once, when I fell off Twister. All the breath got knocked out of me and it almost didn't come back, but then it did and boy was I glad to see it! Then JT wanted to kill me because it was my fault that he hurt his foot. Then my mom and dad were so mad at me for riding off on Twister that it seemed like they wanted to kill me, too. But not really.

I almost got my ear pierced by Kansas. But my mom interrupted that. I took lots of hair off the dog—so much that my dad, who is allergic to pet hair, wouldn't be allergic to that particular dog.

I guess that my spring break was one long field

trip, only with my family and animals and not with our class. Plus I didn't have to carry my notebook around and take notes. Which was a good thing because I had my hands full! I still learned stuff, just like on a real field trip, though.

I learned that people are like barbed wire. They can be prickly but still have their good *points*. (Get it??? My friend Kansas taught me that one!) And I learned why the spark part of spark plugs is important. It's the thing that gets things going. Which is kind of like me! But don't tell JT I said that because he'd probably start calling me Sparky Margaret or Mary Sparkaret or something even dumber.

And "I learned it's wrong to ride off on a horse that's not yours without permission and without telling anyone where you are on the night of a big party—or on any night for that matter. It's wrong and irresponsible and in the future I will use better judgment." (I know this part is yawnfully boring, but my mom made me write it down exactly like that, which is why it's in quotes, so please don't take away points.)

The best thing I got was a friend named Kansas, who I liked then got mad at then liked again after a bunch of stuff happened, but I think I might have already mentioned her. And that's all, so this is . . . THE END!